Th...

Born to i...

Vennor, Eaton, Cassian and Inigo grew up together
on the coasts of Cornwall, knowing that one day
they would inherit their fathers' weighty titles and
the responsibility that comes with being a duke.

When Vennor's father is shockingly murdered, that
day comes sooner than expected. All four heirs
are forced to acknowledge that their lives are
changing. But the one change these powerful
men might not be expecting? Love!

Enjoy this tension-filled new quartet
by Bronwyn Scott

Read Eaton's story in
The Secrets of Lord Lynford

Read Cassian's story in
The Passions of Lord Trevethow

Read Inigo's story in
The Temptations of Lord Tintagel

And look for Vennor's story

Coming soon!

Author Note

Inigo and Audevere's story is about coming to terms with the past. They share loss and they share a personal guilt over their parts in that loss. They wonder if they can ever move forward from the past or if they are forced to define their futures through it. Their story explores what it means to act on the old phrase "burn the ships" and if that is even possible.

It's also a story about the courage to take second chances. The setting for the story gives us a chance to connect with other characters from the series and we get a look at how their second chances are going: we check in with Eaton and Eliza, with Rosenwyn and Cador, and we have news from Cassian and Penrose on their honeymoon. We also get to spend some time with Vennor in London. While the former characters are doing well with their second chances, Vennor seems stranded in the past, unable, like Inigo, to move on from tragedy. These provide potent juxtapositions against which Inigo's story and choices play out.

I think this story resonates with readers because we've all needed a second chance, needed forgiveness from ourselves and others.

BRONWYN SCOTT

The Temptations of Lord Tintagel

Recycling programs for this product may not exist in your area.

ISBN-13: 978-1-335-50546-0

The Temptations of Lord Tintagel

Copyright © 2020 by Nikki Poppen

This edition published by arrangement with Harlequin Books S.A.

For questions and comments about the quality of this book, please contact us at CustomerService@Harlequin.com.

Harlequin Enterprises ULC
22 Adelaide St. West, 40th Floor
Toronto, Ontario M5H 4E3, Canada
www.Harlequin.com

Printed in U.S.A.

Bronwyn Scott is a communications instructor at Pierce College in the United States and the proud mother of three wonderful children—one boy and two girls. When she's not teaching or writing, she enjoys playing the piano, traveling—especially to Florence, Italy—and studying history and foreign languages. Readers can stay in touch via Facebook or on her blog, bronwynswriting.Blogspot.com. She loves to hear from readers.

Books by Bronwyn Scott

Harlequin Historical

Scandal at the Midsummer Ball
"The Debutante's Awakening"
Scandal at the Christmas Ball
"Dancing with the Duke's Heir"

The Cornish Dukes

The Secrets of Lord Lynford
The Passions of Lord Trevethow
The Temptations of Lord Tintagel

Allied at the Altar

A Marriage Deal with the Viscount
One Night with the Major
Tempted by His Secret Cinderella
Captivated by Her Convenient Husband

Russian Royals of Kuban

Compromised by the Prince's Touch
Innocent in the Prince's Bed
Awakened by the Prince's Passion
Seduced by the Prince's Kiss

Visit the Author Profile page
at Harlequin.com for more titles.

To Scott, who got me through this book
as he gets me through so much else.

Chapter One

London—September 1824

The Jilt was getting married. Five years after her last attempt and she was going after a peer. Again. At least that was what it looked like from the society columns and they tended to have the right of it most times. Inigo Vellanoweth set aside the morning edition and took a bracing swallow of hot coffee, searing, strong and bitter, to match the news. It had been bound to happen. Perhaps the surprise was that it hadn't happened sooner, but it did not lessen the shock of seeing it in print. Print lent a certain official quality to information. Print made rumours into facts. Inigo had been following these particular rumours all Season, every mention of *her* with the upstanding Viscount Tremblay buried beneath the larger twin excitements of the Season: the arrival and subsequent death of the Hawaiian King and Cassian Truscott's courtship of Penrose Prideaux. According to *The Times*, the arrangement between the Jilt and Tremblay was all but done. An offer from the Viscount was expected soon. In September, when most of London was absent to protest or to raise the old rumours about her background. Did no one else see her father's calculation in that?

A hundred different questions assailed Inigo as he read, mixed with emotions he would rather not acknowledge. He didn't want to think about her, about the past where their lives had intersected, about his own failures when it came to her and her nefarious father. His reaction to the news was complicated to say the least. Among the myriad questions running through his mind was whether or not she meant marriage this time, or was this another opportunity to ruin a peer? She might mean to go through with it. After all, she was twenty-two now, no longer as young as she'd once been, and Viscount Tremblay, her most recent conquest, was a serious man. A good match by all standards. But the Jilt had made a good match before in Collin Truscott, second son of the Duke of Hayle—an extraordinary match for the daughter of a newly minted knight of the realm. When Sir Gismond Brenley climbed ladders, he did so with ambition and alacrity, using everything and everyone at his disposal—including his own daughter, the exquisite Audevere.

Even now, with five years of tragedy and deceit to tarnish the once-golden debutante, even when he *knew* to be wary of her charms, Inigo could still see her in his mind's eye as she'd once been: her blonde head thrown back, her neck exposed as she laughed, a deep, throaty sound that made a man think of decadence and candlelight, of taking down all that carefully coiffed hair pin by pearl pin. He remembered the way her green eyes would flirt and flash, sharp with intelligence and wit, how her gaze would slide towards Collin, a secret half-smile on her lips that suggested something private just between them even though they were surrounded by a ballroom crowd.

Oh, how he'd envied Collin Truscott, his friend—one of his *best* friends—in those early days! Deep in his heart, Inigo had wanted that for himself: a woman who looked at him the way Audevere had looked at Collin; a woman who could make him laugh with her wit, who had intelligence and who wasn't afraid to use it, unlike the usual debutante thrust in the path of eligible dukes' heirs. Inigo pushed back from the table and began to pace, his body and mind agitated by memories. But Jermyn Street bachelor quarters didn't leave much room to outrun the truth.

In his darker, more honest moments, Inigo admitted it wasn't that he'd wanted *a* woman with whom he could share such moments. He'd wanted *her.* He'd wanted Audevere, his friend's fiancée. It had shamed him then and it still shames him now, because she was not innocent in all her father's ruthless schemes; she bore her share of responsibility for Collin's death. Only his fantasies held back that truth. In them, she was an unwitting accomplice, unaware of the depth of her father's corruption, sometimes even a victim, forced against her will to aid her father's plots. He'd fallen into the habit years ago of making excuses for her and for himself.

No matter how often he'd told himself that such coveting was a sin, that jealousy was poorly done of him, he'd not been able to shake the wanting of her. It was petty of him, he knew. He was the heir and son to the Duke of Boscastle. He was a man who had wealth galore and Midas's own touch for turning a respectable accumulation of money into wealth *unimaginable*. He had everything and yet he'd been jealous of Collin, a man who would never inherit a title, who would always walk in the shadows of others and who had no business sense at all; a man who had only his good looks and winning personality to recommend him and who would always be reliant on his family's connections and wealth for his own livelihood.

But that logic had held little sway with a twenty-five-year-old in desperate, secret love. He'd been privately envious of Collin right up until the day Collin had swum out to the Beasts off the shores of Porth Karrek and promptly drowned, one week to the day after Audevere had broken their engagement and two weeks after Collin's latest business venture with Audevere's father had failed dramatically, costing people homes and jobs they couldn't afford to lose. Collin's family had called it death by misadventure, but those closest to Collin knew better. Between them, father and daughter, the Brenleys had broken him.

And they would pay for it. Inigo had vowed the night of Collin's death to bring Brenley down so that no one else would fall prey to such corruption, such scheming. That had been the beginning of his investigation, five years of piecing together a dirty trail of money that followed Gismond Brenley everywhere he went if anyone cared to look closely enough. Most did not. Did it matter? Brenley was careful. He did nothing illegal, just distasteful, depending on one's politics.

Inigo's pacing halted in mid-thought. Did Tremblay know to look close enough to be suspect of his impending father-in-law? Did Tremblay know to look behind the scenes of the glorious heroics in the Napoleonic Wars that had led to Brenley's knighthood? Or to the sudden acquisition of wealth when Brenley's properties benefited from Parliament's decision to put roads through certain villages and not others? Did Tremblay understand the importance of pushing Brenley off the board of the Blaxford Mining Corporation last year before he could establish a monopoly on Cornish mining? Did Tremblay know all these things and simply not care? This seemed unlikely to Inigo, given the type of man Tremblay was—conscientious and civically minded. Or was Tremblay walking in blind, as Collin had? Blinded by Audevere's beauty, willing to overlook the com-

mon antecedents of her pedigree and all the dirti-
ness that went with it?

Inigo's pacing started anew with a different line
of agitation to pursue. His mind tried to reason that
there was no call for extreme alarm. Surely, Tremblay's solicitors would have done some investigating
of their own. But Inigo was uncomfortable relying
only on assumptions. He'd assumed Collin would be
all right once, too. That was another question raised
by the morning's news. Should he warn Tremblay?

It would require the airing of dirty laundry not
his own—sharing the secrets of the Truscott family. Inigo was protective of his friends. He would not
willingly cause them pain by bringing up a death
they'd taken great care to attribute to an accidental
drowning. Perhaps there was a way to warn Tremblay without exposing the Truscotts to resurrected
scandal? He owed Tremblay full disclosure. The Viscount was a friend. Not to speak up when he had the
power to make a difference would be to serve that
friendship poorly and it ran antithetical to the code of
honour held by the Cornish Dukes—the seven men
he admired most in this world and the next.

Inigo strode into the small room that served as
his study and pulled a set of journals off the shelves
which contained the results of his investigation.
His mind was determined. He had failed Collin. He
would not fail another friend. He would meet with
Tremblay, perhaps invite him to drinks at White's,

and warn him away from a disastrous choice before history could repeat itself.

'I expect Tremblay will want to discuss marriage when we meet this afternoon at Tattersall's.' The words washed over Audevere Brenley, cold and relentless as the Cornish sea in winter. Her father was too confident about his edict for her tastes and that frightened her with good reason, although she gave none of that fear away. It was too early in the day for that. Fear and breakfast did not mix.

'Shouldn't he be discussing marriage with me? After all, you're not the one he wishes to wed.' She sipped her morning tea—a strong Ceylon black—with all the nonchalant sangfroid she could summon. She had been here before, metaphorically speaking. Here at this critical juncture, a pawn advanced in a king's gambit and now it was time for the trap to fall, for the pawn to be sacrificed in fulfilment of her service. She did not want to be here in London, bait once more in her father's attempt to secure a title for the Brenley line. A title his grandchildren could inherit and, until then, a title he could manipulate in Parliament. She wanted to be in Cornwall, away from marriage proposals she didn't want from unsuspecting men who had little idea what a disaster marriage to her would be; men who only saw the beautiful Audevere, the heiress named for an ancient sixth-century Merovingian queen. Her money was *nouveau*; her name was old.

Her father dismissed her remark with a casual wave of his hand. 'Tremblay knows the real business of matrimony is conducted with the father. Asking you is just ceremonial window dressing.'

'What a lovely notion.' Audevere speared him with a sharp tone and a sardonic gaze that conveyed all she thought of such an arrangement. 'Why should my opinion matter? It's only the rest of my life that is being arranged.' He'd been arranging men for her since she was sixteen. It should have been the first sign of his corruption, but she'd been too naive and too flattered at the beginning to understand, desperate as she had been back then to earn her absent father's approval. He'd been at sea most of her life and suddenly he was the only family she had.

'Damn right, gel.' Her father pointed the tines of his fork at her. 'A life that is being arranged to great satisfaction. You will be a lady, the Viscountess of a peer of the realm. Not bad for a man who only made his money a few years ago. Look how far and how fast we've risen. Have I not done well?' Her father flung his arms outwards as if to embrace the room and every last one of its expensive, if not tasteful, trappings.

'Yes, you've done well,' Audevere offered a polite smile. There was no use arguing with him when he was like this—obstinate and confident, assured of his own inviolability. He had achieved much in just seven short years since acquiring his knighthood, but at what cost? Five years ago, her first fiancé,

Collin Truscott, second son of the Duke of Hayle, took his own life in the wake of her father's avarice. Now, a viscount was in her father's sights, waiting to be devoured in the same way—through a marital alliance. History was repeating itself and it was time for it to stop.

'Look what five years have bought us, Daughter.' Her father refilled his plate. No matter how much money he had, he still ate like a man who wasn't sure where the next meal was coming from. 'Perhaps this is Providence's recompense for losing the Duke's son. Truscott was never going to have a title, but Tremblay is already in possession of his. A viscount is a much better trade than a duke's second son. Of course, my own title was new back then. Truscott was the best we could have hoped for back then, but now we've attained even better.'

Audevere pushed her plate away, her appetite dampened by her father's callous disregard for Collin and for her own feelings. She'd cared for the young man. She'd genuinely mourned him. She still remembered with vivid accuracy the day she'd heard the news. Cassian Truscott, the heir, had ridden to Truro in the wind and the rain to tell them the news. She'd been summoned to her father's office where Cassian had waited, drenched, water streaming in rivulets from his greatcoat on to her father's expensive carpet, his expression devastated as he told her.

'Collin is dead. He drowned off the shores of Porth Karrek.'

Cassian had imparted the words with a stern, condemning stare which she had understood implicitly. Collin had drowned *deliberately*. She'd broken with her fiancé and he'd taken his own life. This was her fault. No one went swimming alone in the cold Cornish seas in April. Cassian left shortly after. The moment the door closed behind him, she'd broken into tears, but her father had cursed. 'Damn it all, a Season wasted. We've lost the Duke.'

That day she'd seen him plain, for the first time in his entirety, for what he truly was: an unscrupulous opportunist, ready to rise on the back of anyone who could lift him higher. Even his own daughter. She'd known it in her heart for a few years, but had not wanted to admit it. What daughter did? Life was not sacred to him and in the wake of Collin's death she had hated him for it and had taken no pains to hide it, prompting his disclosure of a secret that devastated what remained of her life.

A secret that would keep her tethered to him.

A secret that meant she would never be free as long as she stayed.

She'd come to understand in hindsight that his damning disclosure had been revealed out of fear she would run. Now she not only hated him, she feared him. In truth, she hated herself for letting that fear rule her, for being powerless to change that fear, powerless to stop him; for being afraid of what would happen to her or anyone she was close to if she tried. But no more. It was time to set aside her fear and take her chances.

'Might I be excused, Father?' A footman came to hold her chair and she rose. 'I have correspondence to see to. So many people are not in London these days.' It was a subtle reminder that for the truly fashionable, the Season had closed long ago, and they ought to be at the town house in Truro.

Her father waved her off and she escaped up to her rooms, gladly shutting her bedroom door behind her. She could have written letters in the lady's parlour at the back of the house, but she felt safer up here, away from the prying eyes of the servants who were instructed to watch her every move, away from her father who endlessly plotted his social ascent, and away from the 'gentlemen' who called on him for business. Out of sight was out of mind and she preferred to be as far from her father's thoughts and friends as possible—although today's news about Tremblay proved that there was nowhere far enough from her father's machinations.

The years since Collin's death had bought her time, but not much else. During her second Season, his death had been a protective shield. No one had approached her out of respect for her mourning and there'd been nothing her father could do about it without looking like a cad. Her third Season had been clouded by rumours of her father's underhanded business dealings regarding the Blaxford Mining Corporation in Cornwall. He'd clashed with the Cor-

nish Dukes and come out the lesser for it. No one
had been interested in courting her then, much to her
father's chagrin. But *ton*nish memories were short.
This year, she'd caught the eye of Viscount Tremblay
and her father had entrenched, running roughshod
over her efforts to quell the Viscount's attentions,
knowing full well that she would be worth less to
him next year. A girl in her fifth Season was as good
as on the shelf; everyone would be wary of a girl who
hadn't taken yet.

Audevere sat at the delicate, white writing desk at
her window overlooking the town house gardens. She
closed her eyes and rubbed her temples, the beginnings of a headache starting to take root as the blood
in her veins thrummed another urgent tattoo: *time
to go, time to go*. It was past time to put a stop to her
father using her in his manoeuvrings. Time to stop
doing his bidding. She was twenty-two years old, no
longer a seventeen-year-old girl whose youth and naivety could excuse her for not having acted sooner.
Time to stop being helpless. No one was going to
ride to her rescue. She would have to rescue herself.

If she meant to act, the time was certainly now,
before another man fell victim to her father. If she
did nothing, she'd be married to Tremblay by New
Year and, perhaps worse than that, she'd be complicit
in her father's schemes this time, knowing full well
ahead of time how he intended to use her. But how
could she stop her father, when he had a list of men
in his pocket who owed him favours, another list of

men who feared blackmail, when he had ruthlessly amassed favours and fortunes that no one dared contest?

The answer was that one person alone could not. There was no hope there. She had done all she could to put Tremblay off without her father finding out, but it seemed he was intent on proposing. She could do nothing there, so she would have to prevent the wedding itself. One could not marry what was not there to be wed. If she were gone, Tremblay at least would be saved. And—a desperate part of her reignited the forlorn hope—*you would be free. At last.*

Freedom would come at a cost, though. Where would she go? There was no one to turn to, no safe place to go. On the one hand, the world was her oyster; she could go anywhere, be anyone, do anything. On the other, the world was a dangerous place for a woman alone with limited resources, a woman who would have to give up everything—even her name—and disappear. She supposed she could give the servants the slip. She could go for a walk and never come back. She could slide out into the world with nothing more than the clothes on her back and whatever she could shove into her pockets. But that was an ominous beginning that begged for failure.

Audevere gazed out over the gardens, finely manicured to perfection even in autumn by her father's gardeners. It would take courage to leave this. Her father's ill-gotten gains had surrounded her in luxuries not easily given up. She'd been enjoying them long before she'd realised people had suffered to create this lifestyle for her.

She drew a steadying breath. She would not let uncertainty hold her back any longer. She could not go on like this, her inaction making her complicit in her father's schemes. Evil prospered when bystanders did nothing but watch and in her mind she was more than a bystander. She could no longer use the excuse that she hadn't known what he was about. She needed help; she needed a friend. But perhaps she would have to settle for an ally. Just one person who would help her get away. One person who wouldn't betray her to her father because they knew what he was and they would believe her when she said her father made her life a living hell, hellish enough to turn her back on it entirely.

Audevere took out a sheet of paper and drew a line down the centre. On the left side she wrote down the characteristics she needed her ally to have: trustworthy, brave, sympathetic and crucially able and willing to keep her secret. On the right side she made a list of friends. When it proved to be short, she added acquaintances. When that also proved to be a rather limited list, she added anyone she knew who wasn't in business or beholden to her father. Totalled, even with those efforts, her list only tallied twelve people and one of them was dead. That left eleven.

She put the first four through the criteria, each failing on some ground in turn. The last seven had something in common. They'd all known Collin:

his family, his mentors, his friends—and for a time they'd been her friends, too, by association. For a while, she'd been part of his close-knit, loving circle. She'd known what it was like to be part of the circle of Cornish Dukes. Would they still acknowledge her? Take her in as their own even though she'd broken her engagement with Collin? She had not seen them since Collin's death. She'd had no contact with them and they had not reached out to her. It seemed ludicrous to think they'd do anything for her, but this was a desperate hour.

Audevere studied the remaining names, hesitating. Eaton Falmage had a family; her father had been a party to an attempt on Eaton's wife's life last year. She could not ask him. She struck a line through his name. Cassian Truscott was out of the country on his honeymoon. Another name from the sacred circle gone. Vennor Penlerick, the new Duke of Newlyn, was still grieving the loss of his father. That left one name: Inigo Vellanoweth, the man who'd once told her quite plainly to her face she wasn't good enough to marry Collin. It wasn't exactly a rousing endorsement for an ally, but it was all she had.

Inigo Vellanoweth met all her criteria and he was rumoured to still be in town. He'd faced down her father over the Blaxford Mines last year and he'd won. Perhaps his desire for continued revenge against her father would win out over his dislike of her. She'd never know unless she asked. She took out another sheet of paper and began to write, a simply worded request to meet tomorrow night at the Bradfords' ball. It would be an innocuous occasion. Now all she needed to do was slip into the back garden and hand a few pence to a street urchin to have the note delivered.

Courage started here. Courage started today.

Chapter Two

Courage, it appeared, required patience. She'd not bargained on that. And patience required nerves of steel in order to act as if nothing had changed. Only a day after sending the note to Inigo, she was already having difficulty with both. She paced her room ceaselessly and found herself jumping at the slightest sound. Her senses seemed fine-tuned to the smallest nuance. Even now she heard the front door open downstairs. Her father was home. She had not seen him since breakfast yesterday. He was sure to have news. She braced herself against what the news might be *and* the bellow that was sure to come. Once a sea captain, always a sea captain. She counted down: three, two, one. And on cue…

'Audevere!' Her father's voice boomed up the grand staircase of Brenley House, echoing off the wainscoted ceilings, as if he were still on the deck of a ship. Audevere cringed against the invasion of the noise and what it might portend. She glanced at her little clock. If only time went faster! It seemed an age until tonight's ball. She was ready for that at least. She'd rehearsed her words, the lines she wanted to say; she'd anticipated each argument Inigo might make. And he *would* argue.

They'd been good at arguing. Once, she'd looked forward to sparring with Inigo. He had a quick wit and a sharp mind, though with a darker shade compared to Collin's light. The remembrance of those arguments brought a faint smile to her lips even as her father's voice bellowed up the stairs again. 'Audevere, come down here at once!' Her father might wear the mask of a gentleman, dress in a gentleman's clothes and live in a gentleman's house, but he would always be a sea captain. He expected to be obeyed instantaneously. She'd learned quickly not to ignore a summons from her father, even though one was seldom summoned for good news.

She found him in his office, standing before the massive, polished mahogany desk from which he conducted all his business, legs spread apart, shoulders straight, hands behind his back. 'Father, what has happened?' She put on a mask of interest to cover her nerves. She hoped her note had not been discovered, that she'd not been called down here to be punished.

He smiled broadly and some of her fears eased. Her little subterfuge was safe. 'I've brought you a gift, that's what's happened.' He gestured towards the large dressmaker's box, sitting on the low table before the sofa. It was tied with a trademark ribbon of pale-pink satin attached to a black card trimmed in gilt, marking the box as coming from one of the finest drapers in London.

'For me?' Audevere fingered the soft satin lovingly even as her mind was already on alert. This was an expensive and unexpected gift. The ribbon alone cost a worker's wages for a month. She'd been fifteen when her father had begun his rise to fortune, old enough to remember life before the knighthood, before wealth permitted her to forgo counting pennies and questioning the need for fripperies, too young to realise the price of her father's fortune.

'Well, go on, girl. Open it and see if it suits.' Her father waved at the box impatiently, and perhaps with a bit of pride in being able to shop at such an establishment. Even after seven years, that particular thrill had not faded for him, although it had for her. No matter how pretty the ribbon or the box, no gift from her father or his friends came without strings attached. She'd learned that lesson the hard way— through painful experience.

Ever wary, Audevere untied the ribbon and carefully laid it aside. There were yards of it, enough for her to do something clever with and still have some left to give her maid. Patsy was perhaps her one friend within the walls of Brenley House. She would be in alt over the ribbon. Audevere lifted the lid and reached into the depths of white tissue paper. Despite her caution, her breath couldn't help but catch as she drew out the gown. 'Oh! It's lovely!'

She held the gown against herself, shaking out the skirts. Lovely was an understatement. Cranberry silk shimmered beneath an overskirt of soft ivory lace, a wide cranberry ribbon banded the waist. The gown was a tribute to autumn. Audevere could only imagine the hours that had gone into making the yards of lace for the overskirt. Once, she'd never dreamed of owning such a fine gown.

She spun in a quick circle, letting herself pretend for a moment that she had a normal father who would spoil his daughter because he loved and cared for her, that this gown was a gift she could enjoy without shame, without guilt, without fear. 'I'll wear it tonight at the Bradfords' ball.' The words had barely left her mouth when the fantasy was over.

'I was hoping you would. I had ordered it in expectation of announcing your engagement—' condescending disappointment edged his words '—but now we need the gown to do battle or we'll lose the Viscount.' Ah. The agenda at last. She'd suspected nothing less. But the news behind it was a surprise.

'*Lose* him?' Audevere looked up from admiring the dress. 'Did something happen at Tattersall's?' She put the pretty dress back in the box with a sigh— a beautiful gown in exchange for an ugly favour that would advance his plans. She was pleased the Viscount seemed to have slipped her father's hook, yet now she was needed yet again to grease the gears of her father's advancement.

'Tremblay didn't come. Can you imagine that? He sent a note saying he was delayed by business matters.' Her father's features were hard. 'Of course, I wanted to know why when he knew very well what the point of today's meeting was. I discovered what those business matters were: afternoon drinks with Inigo Vellanoweth at White's. Now he refuses to receive me. I asked for an appointment this morning and was denied. He insults both you and me with this behaviour.' His fist came down hard on the surface of his desk, the inkpot jumping. 'All summer we worked on this and this is how Tremblay treats me? I am a knight of the realm!' It always came back to this. His title, his wants. Audevere had never known a more self-focused individual or a more dangerous one.

Audevere's mind ran over her father's revelation and all it could mean. A thrill shot through her at the thought: *drinks with Inigo.* Was it because of her note? Or had he not received it by then? She wished she knew. Timing was everything. If it was after her note arrived, it meant he'd agreed to help her and had gone immediately into action on her behalf. But if the meeting had occurred beforehand, it meant something entirely different—that he meant to meddle, perhaps for the purpose of striking a blow for vengeance against her father. Did that blow include her? Was his hate still so strong after five years that he wanted to strike at her, too? The latter interpretation of his meeting with Tremblay boded ill for the evening. She would have to tread carefully.

'You need to get Tremblay back,' her father was saying. 'Tintagel is whispering poison in his ear.' It was proof of her father's anger that he referred to Inigo by his title. 'Tonight, you dance with Tremblay, you flirt with him, you take him out on the veranda and kiss him. Find a few trustworthy friends to witness it if that's what it takes,' he growled. 'We need the Viscount to come up to scratch. We need his proposal before he decides to leave town or before Tintagel ruins this like he ruined the Blaxford deal. I'll be damned if we let him slip away now. We'll look like desperate fools.' He paused. 'What? You look appalled. It's nothing you haven't done before,' he dismissed her distaste.

No, it wasn't, more was the pity, the guilt, the shame. She'd been cajoling his friends and business partners since she was sixteen. How many times had she flattered a man until he felt important, all so her father could win contracts, close deals and lead the less discerning astray? Not this time, Audevere vowed silently. It wouldn't hurt to dance with the Viscount tonight, but she would not force his hand and she would not be dragged to the altar. If she'd had any lingering doubts about running or about approaching Inigo for help, this confirmed her choice. She had to act now and tonight at the ball was her chance to strike a bargain with Inigo. The old tattoo beat its rhythm more insistently than ever. *Time to go, time to go.* 'I don't like the idea of forcing Tremblay's hand.'

'We're not forcing Tremblay to do anything.' Her father smiled coldly. 'We're just helping him to remember why he likes you so much.' He moved towards her, giving her a chuck under the chin. 'Do I need to remind you of all that is at stake?'

It was a polite way of subtly cataloguing his threat against her, of what he would expose if she refused to abet his efforts. She did not think he would hesitate to do it either. He was not a good father. He'd been very careful to make sure she had no way out, no friends to turn to, no independence of her own. But now, if she were willing to risk it, perhaps it could be different. Perhaps, for the first time, she could wriggle out of his stranglehold. If she was brave. *Courage starts today.* The mantra had taken up a place beside the other one that ran through her head. *Time to go, time to go.*

He smiled with what passed as paternal benevolence. 'Don't fail me, my dear.' The reminder was there in his tone, the message clear beneath the calm demeanour. She'd already failed him once. She couldn't afford another dead aristocrat.

Audevere was here. After five years of avoiding her, she was now merely across the room. His memories of her had failed to do her justice. Inigo's gaze followed Audevere about the ballroom, pausing when she paused, moving when she moved, taking in all the details of her: her hair was paler, her chin sharper, her green eyes brighter, her classical beauty more emphasised than it had been years earlier. Perhaps it was the staid company kept by the Bradfords that caused her to glitter so stunningly, or perhaps she would take his breath away wherever she was, whomever she was among, whatever she had done. He couldn't let himself forget the last. She'd had a hand in Collin's fate. That knowledge had kept him angry for years. He couldn't set it aside now at the first sight of her, no matter how poignant her plea.

Her note was in his pocket. Short and concise.

I need your help.

The word 'need' was underlined twice for emphasis. What kind of emphasis? Desperation? Urgency? He touched his pocket, feeling the folded paper inside. Did she truly need help? Or was this note part of a vengeful plot hatched in retaliation for the Blaxford deal? He wouldn't know unless he showed up.

Meet me at the Bradford ball. I will come to you.

The irony was that he'd been likely to meet her here anyway. Tremblay had invited him to come along and he'd thought it a good idea to keep his friend in his sights after their meeting at White's. Apparently, Brenley was of the same mind. Brenley had not left the Viscount's side all night. That was unnerving. Brenley did not mean to let Tremblay go without a fight and Gismond Brenley was doggedly tenacious.

Inigo took a moment away from watching Audevere and studied the two men standing together. He wondered what it was that Brenley wanted so desperately from Tremblay? Inigo had his guesses. A pocket peer in the House of Lords whom Brenley could manipulate? Or was he after Tremblay's extensive sugar plantation holdings in the West Indies? Was it something else Inigo didn't know about— although he couldn't imagine what that might be. He'd thoroughly investigated the man. He liked to think he knew everything there was to know about Brenley's holdings, the good—of which there was not much—and the bad—of which there was plenty.

The orchestra had taken a short intermission and Inigo used the opportunity to step outside for fresh air. The ball, while certainly not a crush—the Season was too far behind them for that—was full enough to be warm and he welcomed the cool air on his face, although he doubted others would. The chill would keep most people indoors. The veranda would be private. He'd give Audevere another hour to make her approach—more than enough time—and then he would leave. Perhaps he would persuade Tremblay to leave with him. They could stop at the club for a night cap. He could be in bed by midnight. Damn, but London out of Season was slow. It was past time to go home to Cornwall.

If it weren't for this business of watching over Tremblay, he'd be in Cornwall by now, enjoying autumn on the coast with his friends—or what remained of them. Cassian Truscott, Collin's older brother, was abroad and Vennor Penlerick refused to leave London. But the Trelevens were there, and the Kittos, as were Eaton and Eliza. There was the autumn recital to look forward to at the Kittos' conservatory, truffle hunting in the woods with Eaton, and he wanted to check on Eliza's mining schools to see the progress the children were making.

He was bone-tired of London, something he'd once thought impossible. London was less exciting now that Eaton and Cassian were married, choosing to spend the bulk of their time in Cornwall. Cassian could be excused—he was on his honeymoon— but when he came back, he would not waste time in town. Of their foursome, there was only Vennor Penlerick left. It had been over a year since Richard Penlerick and his wife had been killed coming home from the theatre. But Vennor's grief was as deep as ever. At what point did one tell a friend it was time to get on with the business of living? Who had that right? Did he, when he still grieved for Collin? When he still sought to protect the world from the corruption of Sir Gismond Brenley? Who was he to tell Vennor to set aside his grief, to not let it consume him?

Inigo leaned on the stone balustrade of the veranda and looked out into the dark, unlit garden. Maybe that was his problem, too: he had let grief consume him where the others had not. Eaton and Cassian had found ways to live again, to love again. He hadn't and now he was alone in his grief, isolated in his vendetta against Brenley just as Vennor was increasingly isolated in his search for his parents' killer. That didn't mean his cause wasn't just. It only meant it was exacting more than he'd anticipated. The French doors opened behind him, casting a sliver of light on his slice of the veranda. He stiffened in anticipation and was not disappointed.

'I thought I might find you out here. You always did like dark corners.' He'd recognise those low-throated tones anywhere. Audevere Brenley had been blessed with a voice meant for seduction. Her scent met him on the air; it was the sweet spice of amber mixed with nutmeg. She smelled of autumn and memories.

Inigo turned, leaning back against the balustrade, allowing himself to take in the full beauty of her up close, her pale gold hair piled high, her long neck on display, her body dressed to its fullest potential in cranberry silk and ecru lace. 'I received your note.' It had been waiting for him when he returned from White's.

'Thank you for coming,' she said easily, joining him at the rail as if they were still old friends. 'It's been a long time, Inigo.' She favoured him with a soft smile that caught him off guard. He'd assumed since he'd couched their present relationship in adversarial terms that she did, too. Apparently that was not the case, or she was playing with him. He must always be alert to that possibility.

'Too long, perhaps.' There was censure in his tone to indicate it had been too long for first names. Perhaps it had been that way before when they'd been carefree, but no longer. Too much had happened between them. They were not friends. Not any more, if they ever truly had been.

She nodded in acknowledgement. 'Perhaps. Forgive me for my forwardness; there is much at stake and I haven't time for civilities.'

Inigo gave her a strong stare. She was different this evening—conciliatory, conspiratorial even. It was unlike her and he was instantly wary. 'Is that your strategy? To woo information from me with sweetness? Did your father send you out here to beg information on the pretence of renewing old acquaintances?'

Her smile faded and some of her sweetness, too. His words had stung. 'I came of my own accord. My father does not suspect I've sought you out. I hoped there might at least be honesty left between us.'

'Then you would do better to ask me directly for whatever it is you want to know. Let's not pretend you don't know I met with Tremblay yesterday, or why I did so.' Inigo watched her face harden, the mask of softness slipping from it into an expression he was more familiar with: sharpness. She was never more brilliant than when she was cornered.

'Very well. Let me be direct. Are you attempting to interfere with my betrothal?'

Inigo gave a dry laugh. 'That's a bit hasty since there is no betrothal. Tremblay has not proposed.'

'Not yet. But I had reason to believe he would, right up until yesterday.' She slanted him a sideways glance, 'Unless you've managed to dissuade him? I recall you were always very good at persuasion.'

'Do you wish to marry him?' A moment's guilt swept him. Perhaps he was interfering with more than Brenley's arrangements. Perhaps, by warning off Tremblay, he was interfering with her personal happiness, with her plan for escaping the clutches of her scheming father? It was difficult to think of Audevere Brenley as being entitled to her own happiness. She'd been the enemy for so long, she and her father. But she'd not always been his enemy. She'd once been something else quite wonderful and he'd liked her, admired her. There were other stronger descriptors he could use, but they admitted too much. Whatever those descriptors, it seemed his feelings weren't altogether defeated. He didn't want to feel empathy for her. Collin was dead because of her. 'It is certainly my business if you think to ruin another good man.'

She looked genuinely wounded at the claim. She'd not missed his implication. 'That was never my intention with Collin. I need you to believe that. I was young and naive. I had no idea what my father was doing until it was too late and I had no idea Collin would—' Her voice broke and she could not manage the words.

Inigo managed them for her. 'Take his own life?' It was important. The words must be said, owned. He would not, could not, pretend this didn't lie between them.

'Yes,' she managed to say the single word with soft feeling. 'He was so full of life, so full of happiness, it never occurred to me he would do such a thing. Up until then, I think I believed he was in some way untouchable, that the world couldn't reach him.' She shook her head. 'I see now it was naive of me.'

'It's hard to imagine you as naive, so forgive me if I reserve judgement.' He'd expected her to be insulted by the insinuation, to flash a show of her hot temper, slap him even in her defence. His jaw was braced for it. Perhaps he even wanted to see her angry. He understood that person and that person was the enemy. It was harder to reconcile this other person who stood beside him, reflective and penitent, vulnerable in her own way, sharing the loss of Collin. But she did not rail. She touched him and it set his world on fire.

She laid a bold, gloved hand on his dark sleeve, the gesture sending a bolt of the old awareness up his arm, her touch as insistent as her words. 'Whatever else you believe, believe this: I did not want Collin to die.'

No, probably not, Inigo thought uncharitably. That much was true. A dead Collin was no good to her father. A dead Collin was scandalous. There was no profit in scandal for a woman looking to marry well. Perhaps she'd paid for that death, her best Seasons spent shrouded by the knowledge that everyone knew she'd broken the engagement and that her fiancé had died through 'misadventure' shortly afterwards. Now she was finally able to venture forth and try again for a title, the scandal watered down by years of other scandals to diminish and obscure her own. He'd noticed. He'd made it his business to stay abreast of what the Brenleys were up to.

She persisted, seemingly unaware of his cynicism. 'I will live with the guilt of his death for the rest of my life. Perhaps there was some clue I overlooked, perhaps there was some way in which I should have known how breaking the engagement would affect him.' Her confession, so similar to his own—that he should have known, should have foreseen what Collin would do—threatened to convince Inigo she'd cared for Collin in truth. 'That's why I wrote to you, Inigo. That's why I cannot let this marriage to Tremblay go through. I will not be the means by which another good man is ruined.'

The longer she talked, the more she became the girl he'd known and less the enemy he'd cast her as in the years since. Inigo pushed those feelings away ruthlessly. He didn't want to pity her. He didn't want to feel anything for this beauty who had been his friend's undoing. But all the sins he had laid at her doorstep were not quite enough to make her irresistible. He was aware of her nearness, the scent of her, the touch of her, the sound of her, the sight of her. She could not move without him being aware of each nuance. Time had not been his friend in that regard.

'What is it that you need from me?' Inigo asked flatly, aware that in supplying that need he could keep his friend from the danger posed by the Brenleys. It was the devil's own deal, one that would require him to be in close proximity to his greatest temptation.

'I need you to help me get away, to become someone else, to go somewhere I can start over, somewhere my father will never find me, never use me again as a tool to hurt others.' Green eyes flashed in the night, determination and defiance a mask for the fear that he would refuse her. It was a sign of how much the request meant to her, how much courage it had taken to ask. But despite the temptation, his own caution wouldn't allow him to capitulate easily.

'You mean to run away? To vanish? Just like that?' Inigo snapped his fingers. The plan was outrageous. Had she truly thought it through? It wasn't that it couldn't be done, but that he couldn't picture the exquisite Audevere Brenley doing it.

'Yes.' She was holding her breath.

'I am supposed to believe you? That this is not

an elaborate set-up to frame me in a kidnapping or compromise me into marriage? I can imagine your father would find a large amount of vindication in marrying his daughter to one of the Cornish Dukes.' It took brains to remain single when the matchmaking mamas grew ever more creative about ways to set their daughters' caps for him.

'Yes.' Her grip on his arm was a clutching gesture now. 'Please, you have to believe me, Inigo. You are the only one who can help me because you alone know what my father is.'

She was potent like this, irresistible. He should have turned his back on her long before this, should not have answered her summons and given her a chance to persuade him. Being close to her only made it harder to refuse. Hadn't he spent five years avoiding her, and the way she stirred him, out of loyalty for Collin? And here he was, tempted by a few soft words in the moonlight to throw away those efforts and entertain the pleasure of striking a bargain with Audevere Brenley. 'Why do you think I'd be interested in negotiating anything with you?'

'Because you know what my father is. I think you want revenge for Collin. If you could have got that revenge on your own, you would have had it by now—as I would have.' Her eyes were steady on his. 'I need you, Inigo. We need each other. I can't do it alone and neither can you.'

It was masterfully done. How long had she rehearsed that little speech? Rearranged the words to maximum effect? Had she known how his mind would wrap around that those phrases? Had she calculated all the wild inferences his mind would draw from those words? The curiosity it would provoke to see them as allies, not enemies? To realise that they'd been allies all this time?

Audevere Brenley had come out to the veranda wrapped in moonlight and soft words as if the darkness of the past didn't lie between them, for the intention of securing his assistance. What had driven her to this point, where approaching an old nemesis for the purpose of vanishing seemed like her best option? The curiosity was too much. He answered her with a stare of his own and said against his better judgement, 'You have five minutes to make your case.'

Chapter Three

She only needed two of those minutes, which was proof—if he still needed it—that this was a premeditated strategy on her part. She'd not approached him idly. She was in earnest about disappearing. Her eyes were twin green flames burning with her insistence. 'Even if I stop this wedding, it won't be enough. There will be another attempt and another as long as I am here. Help me get away. Help me stop being my father's pawn, for good.'

Her eyes darted away, but not before Inigo saw real fear in her gaze. It gave him pause and generated a genuine concern he'd not expected or wanted to feel for her. She made a compelling case. It was reshaping how he saw her: not as the carefree girl he'd known in her youth, nor as the enemy he'd seen her as after Collin's death. For the first time, he was seeing her as a pawn, a young woman caught in the web of her father's deceit, unable to help herself. But he must go carefully down this new road and look beyond the emotion of her situation. There must be logic to it as well.

'Why not marry Tremblay and let him put an end to your father's pressure? Surely Tremblay's title will protect you if you want to break from your father.' Inigo paused, wanting to be fair. 'Tremblay is fond of you. He cares for you. He would help you.' It was hard to utter that truth when temptation stood before him, rousing all his old demons and desires against his better self, and this time there was no Collin to prevent it. This time, Audevere needed him; *she'd* come to *him*.

Audevere shook her head. 'To marry Tremblay is to ruin him. My father will use me to keep Tremblay close, to force him to use his influence as my father forced Collin. If Tremblay cares for me, it will be even worse. He'll give in to my father, thinking he is protecting me.'

She wanted to protect Tremblay. She was willing to give him up in order to achieve that. Was there real affection there that he had overlooked? Slowly, he asked the awkward question, the answer to which he wasn't sure he wanted to hear. Wanting or not wanting to marry him wasn't the same as loving him. 'Do you love Tremblay?'

She sighed and gave him a sad look. 'What is love, Inigo? Is it the ephemeral passions found in fairy tales? If so, then, no. I don't love him. Is it something less fiery? Something akin to caring, to not wanting to see him brought down by my father's greed and underhanded dealings? Then, yes.'

'Protection is not love.' Inigo crossed his arms over his chest. She protected herself, she sought to protect Tremblay just as he sought to protect his own friends. Before tonight, it was not an attribute he'd thought to have in common with this woman he'd taught himself to look upon as an adventuress. 'Protection is the civility one citizen owes another. It is what keeps society from being entirely corrupt.'

'Protection is what I want from you, Inigo. Tremblay cannot give it to me. He will not want me when this is done. Whatever fondness he believes he feels for me now, he will be glad to have escaped.' She met him with a challenge in her stare. 'Will you give me the protection I seek by helping me vanish?'

Her tone made it clear she wanted an answer tonight. Now. But he could not afford to rush headlong to her defence, no matter how vulnerable she seemed in the moment. Stern stoicism and neutrality were his best weapons out here on the veranda, alone with her—a woman who had learned the art of persuasion at her father's knee and roused him beyond measure. 'I have questions.'

'Then come inside and dance with me. I will answer them. My five minutes is up and people will notice if we remain out here much longer.' It was a skilful manoeuvre. He could see her hope that this would be a slippery slope towards acceptance of her request. What she could not command outright from him, she thought to cajole out of him in slow steps. Was she that sure of her charms or was she that sure of him? The last made him uneasy. While they had been almost constantly in one another's company all those years ago through their association with Collin, surely he was not an open book to her? Surely she did not guess his darkest secret? He kept it well buried. Not even his closest friends had guessed.

'As you wish.' He made her a short bow and ushered her indoors, his hand light at her back as he led her on to the dance floor. He would touch her as little as necessary, although the waltz required far more touching than most dances. Perhaps, his agile, suspicious mind whispered, she understood that most basic aspect of charm: touch persuaded where words might fail. When people touched, they confessed; they capitulated. Touch was dangerous, powerful.

He put a hand to her waist, her own hand resting on his shoulder, comfortable and firm. She slid her other hand into his with an enviable certainty that it belonged there. There were no light, perfunctory touches from her. Sweet heavens, when was the last time a woman had tried this successfully to seduce him? Was that what she was doing or was he doing that all by himself, reading too much into the smallest nuance? It was the price one paid for being a cynic, he supposed. One always had to look at all the angles. One could never take anything at face value.

The music began and he moved them into the dance. One, two, three, one, two, three. She was light in his arms and confident on her feet. He remembered she liked to dance. She knew she was good at it. Eyes that had been dagger sharp on the veranda sparkled with enjoyment now. 'Ask your questions, Inigo. The dance won't last for ever and I don't think we can afford two at this juncture.'

That was the dilemma, of course. What could he really afford with her? Could he afford *not* to believe her? To assume the worst and let her find her own level? On the other hand, could he afford *to* believe her? Beneath her soft words this evening, there was a darker reality. In taking up her offer to thwart Brenley, he was letting her own self-professed naivety exonerate her. Inigo wasn't sure how he felt about that. Was Audevere Brenley manipulating him with her plea or was she as desperate as she seemed behind her bold mask?

'Inigo, I have told you the truth. Why do you resist?' She was all soft, feminine perfection in the asking. For a moment his resolve faltered.

'You want me to help you and yet you jilted my best friend and helped bring about his death. I hardly know what to make of your request. Surely you must see that. You are the daughter of a manipulating tyrant. I must at least entertain the notion that the apple doesn't fall far from the tree.'

Soft femininity dissolved. He'd angered the goddess within again. 'You know nothing of me and what my life has been like. I think it would surprise you greatly. Whatever I have done, I have done for self-preservation.'

'As you do this thing now? This attempt to run from your past?' It was time to lay out his terms. 'If I'm to help you, I need complete honesty. Can you give me that?'

'Yes. What I tell you will be the complete truth.'

Inigo did not miss the slightest of hesitations as she clearly debated with herself over how to define her answer so that it wasn't a lie. 'That's not what I was hoping for, Miss Brenley.' He could tell she sought to retain the right to omit painful truths, but he would not give her that ground. If they were trust each other, he had to know she was not working against him in any way.

She tossed her head, the light of the Bradfords' Venetian chandeliers picking out the diamond chips in her tiara. There it was: more self-preservation. He would test that honesty now. 'Why come to me? Surely our recent past doesn't recommend us as likely allies.' Those were the politest terms he could use to frame the animosity between him and Brenley—and by extension her. Although, it was proving difficult to remember that tonight when faced with this desperate, penitent version of her, this woman who saw, albeit belatedly, the truth of who her father was and what he had done, and her own role, whether unwittingly or not, in facilitating his actions. Was that the truth or a façade?

She was ready for him, 'On the contrary, I think

it makes us the most likely of allies. I want to stop being used as my father's tool and you *hate* Gismond Brenley.'

Hate was an understatement. The man was a murderer in Inigo's opinion. But it wasn't reason enough for her to have sought him, of all people, out, not with the sordid past that lay between them. The canny minx would have to do better than that. 'A lot of people hate Gismond Brenley.' Inigo took them through the next turn with a burst of speed, his hand tightening at her back out of frustrated emotion.

'*You're* not afraid of him, Inigo. That's what makes you different. You stopped him from taking Eliza Blaxland's mines. You were relentless last year on her behalf, but it wasn't enough for you, was it? You still want revenge for Collin.' She paused, whetting her lips. 'You want a life for a life. What could be more fitting than stealing me away from him in retribution for him having stolen Collin from you?'

Dear lord, she saw too much. He wished her gaze would move over his shoulder where it belonged instead of fixed on him with those aventurine eyes, green pools that begged him to drown in them. He imagined when she raged they turned to turbulent whirlpools, sucking down everything in their path. But those eyes were her flaw as well. She was too transparent. A smart man could read her a mile away. She hid nothing if a man was wise enough to look, wise enough to avoid being misled by the sheer beauty of her. He hoped he was wise enough.

Tonight he saw desperation behind her bold words. She was striking hard and fast because her need was real and time was of the essence. At least that was what he wanted to believe.

He turned them at the bottom of the ballroom, cutting past another couple. 'What you're asking for is more than just buying out board members and re-placing them with my own minions. Do you know what it will mean to disappear?'

'It means I will be free. That I can't be used again.' Her chin went up a fraction in defiant antic-ipation of his argument. He did not let the point of that chin deter him.

'It means you will be alone, at the mercy of the world. It means you will be without the luxuries you are used to and no resources beyond your body with which to acquire them.' He spared no mercy in his assessment. She might be stopping one marriage, but she might be setting herself up for a less savoury one.

'I assure you, I know exactly what I'm doing.' Her tones were crisp, fierce. He wondered if she was trying to convince herself as much as she was try-ing to convince him. What she proposed was auda-cious in the extreme. She knew it and she was wise enough to fear it.

'Then you're one step ahead of me,' Inigo rejoin-dered. 'I'm still trying to answer my first question. Why should I join forces with you? You say you can help me achieve revenge, strike out at your father by helping you disappear.' They were running out of time, the dance nearly done. Only one more pass of the ballroom remained to them. 'But the truth is, he cannot know who helped you. It would jeopardise your ability to remain beyond his reach. So, I ask you again. Why should I help you?'

Her eyes glittered dangerously, the only warning he had before she played her ace. 'Because it's the right thing to do. You are the most honourable man I've met and stopping my father is the honourable thing to do. You were Collin's best friend. He would want you to help me.' Her hard emerald eyes softened. 'And if those reasons aren't enough, I would call on one more. Once upon a time, you didn't hate me. Once, despite all your efforts to the contrary, you liked me, just a little, and I would call on the memory of that fondness now in the hour of my greatest need.'

The last of his resolve crumbled. So that was how it was to be: for honour, for loyalty, for love—although she had not called it that, did not guess that she could call it that—he would set aside his misgivings and do her bidding, risky as it was for both of them. There was no guarantee that helping her escape would get her what she wanted.

The waltz ended and Inigo was aware of Brenley's gaze on them. 'Your father is watching us. What will you tell him?' He whispered the words close to her ear, allowing himself the luxury of breathing in the amber-and-nutmeg scent of her.

She smiled, for a moment simultaneously coy and innocent, her eyes only playing at naivety. 'I will tell him I'm trying to bring Viscount Tremblay up to scratch as he's asked and that I'm doing it by waltzing with the most eligible man here.' It wasn't untrue as far as it went. 'He'll like the notion of creating competition.' She squeezed his hand and whispered, 'Inigo, thank you for this. I don't know how I'll ever be able to repay you. When I need you, I'll send word.'

Then she was gone, back to the sidelines, out of his reach until next time, her task a *fait accompli*. He was in bed with his enemy's daughter, his dead best friend's fiancée and a host of ghosts from his past. Heaven help him. He was going to need a bigger bed.

Chapter Four

'You were waltzing with the enemy.' There was nothing like a sharp condemnation from her father to pierce the euphoria of her little victory. His grip dug into the bare flesh of her arm as he tugged her behind a potted palm and out of sight. But Audevere had expected no less. Nothing escaped her father's attention. It was the price she had to pay for securing Inigo's help.

'All aristocrats are your enemy, Father.' She gave a light laugh. 'If I didn't dance with your foes, I'd never dance at all. Don't you always say to keep your friends close and your enemies closer?' She held her breath and waited for his response, watching him carefully for a sign he suspected she was hiding something. He would be ruthless if he thought she was trying to play him false. She was counting on his arrogance to get her through this first hurdle. He was too sure of himself and too sure of her—or rather his hold over her—to doubt her loyalty.

His face relaxed and he chuckled. 'I see I have an apt apprentice in you, my dear. Keeping your enemies close indeed, especially with that one. Tintagel is particularly dangerous, him and those Cornish Dukes.' Her father disliked many men, but at the top of his list were the four Cornish Dukes, men who loved their families, who were devoted to personally raising their heirs and believed it was their duty to provide for the civic welfare of their communities with wide-sweeping projects and reforms that benefitted people, not purses. They were selfless men who put others first. In short, they stood for everything her father despised; they held as ideals the values he saw as weaknesses.

His laugh faded and he eyed her again. 'What business could we have in drawing Tintagel near?' He was testing her, but she was prepared.

'To ensure he doesn't interfere with my betrothal to Tremblay, of course. Now he knows that we know what he tried to do with his meeting at White's. Perhaps now we've gained a little of our own back by driving a wedge between the two friends,' she argued shrewdly, hating herself for the lies, hating even more the ease with which those lies came to her. Inigo's comment about the apple not falling far from the tree smarted. She didn't want him to be right. She was only lying now out of self-preservation. 'Maybe Tremblay will feel there is competition, a challenger who comes from the ranks of his friends, the very friend who tried to warn him away. Perhaps Tremblay will question Tintagel's motives in giving that warning. Perhaps he'll disregard it, thinking that his friend meant to woo me for himself.'

'Very astute, Daughter.' Her father nodded his approval. 'While we're keeping Tintagel close, it wouldn't hurt to winkle out a secret or two. I'd like some leverage over him. Those Cornish Dukes act as if they're squeaky clean, but no one's that spotless. Everyone has skeletons; some people just bury them deeper.'

'I'll see what I can do.' Audevere could hardly say less without arousing suspicion, but her mind was already chanting, *time to go, time to go.* It was past time, really.

He grinned and released her arm. 'You are my daughter in truth; blood will always tell.' She smiled as if his approval was something she coveted and was relieved when he excused himself to the card rooms.

At last she could draw an easy breath; at last she could allow herself a moment's celebration. She'd been brave. She'd put her plan in motion. Inigo Vellanoweth would help her. And in the morning the real work could begin at last. She needed to arrange for what funds she could, convert what she had to cash, decide what to take with her, decide where to go. Audevere was thankful for the solid substance of the wall at her back, for the privacy of the palms that let her slouch with the audacity of her plans. She'd been quick in her answer to Inigo tonight: that she understood the magnitude of her plans and their consequences. She did understand them in theory. It was the practice that was overwhelming.

Her life was about to change drastically. She told herself she wouldn't mind. She'd be free…if she succeeded. If she failed, though, she would not get a second chance. Her father was not built for forgiveness, not even for his own daughter. Succeed or fail, she'd be cut off from her only living family, entirely alone in the world. There was little elation in that thought, although she wasn't certain why it should bother her. Wasn't she already alone? Her father was hardly any type of father at all, but a man who used his daughter to further his own interests, blackmailed her with the fear of having her darkest secrets exposed as if she were just another of his hapless victims, encouraged her to entertain men of his choosing and implicated her in his schemes against her will.

She smoothed her skirts and returned to the ball. She wanted to dance until she forgot her worries. She had partners aplenty and she danced until she was breathless and exhausted. But no partner seemed to match Inigo's skill and yet every partner reminded her of him in what they lacked. Her partners became a string of opposites—they looked decorously away, not daring to meet her gaze, where Inigo's eyes had pierced hers, pale, blue and all-seeing as if they could see into her very soul. She'd forgotten how unique his eyes were, so unique they had their own name—Boscastle blue—handed down from generations of Boscastle dukes. The years had changed

him, honed the young man she'd known who'd preferred dark corners into a handsome, striking man
who would not go unnoticed in any room. He was
a sharp man, too, in all ways. Inigo's words had cut
through to the truth where her other partners made
useless small talk.

Inigo had asked the hard questions. *Why did she
want this? Why had she come to him? Could he trust
her?* That was what he'd really been asking when
he'd insisted she tell him the truth.

It would be hard not to, with those irresistible
blue eyes boring into her. She nodded and smiled at
something her current partner said. It was no challenge to keep up with his conversation even when
she wasn't really listening. She could just nod and
smile and let her mind wander back to Inigo. His eyes
had always mesmerised her, so impenetrable, even
as they sought out her own secrets. One never knew
what he was really thinking. Unlike Collin, whose
thoughts she'd always been able to read. There'd been
charm in Collin's openness, but there was a depth of
mystery in Inigo that could keep a girl up all night
with questions.

She knew. She'd spent more than a few nights
wondering what thoughts lay behind those eyes. It
hadn't been well done of her, thinking about her fiancé's friend, but she consoled herself with the possibility it was just the natural curiosity of a young
girl in the throes of her first taste of courtship. It
was easier to think the latter and she might have

convinced herself it was true if she hadn't seen him again, hadn't danced with him, hadn't felt his hand at her back or the force of his gaze. All the curiosity came surging back, only this time she had more specific words for it, words like longing. Those words were far less innocuous.

Her mind was curious about other things now, too. Had she gone to Inigo strictly because she believed he could get the job done? Or were there other more secret motives that had driven her decision? She needed to tread carefully and be honest with herself on that score. She was attracted to Inigo. She'd rather not be, not when he could so easily be her enemy, nor when the liking would all be one-sided.

If she'd learned one thing from her father's victims, it was never to mix business with pleasure. The only thing that mattered tonight was that Inigo had agreed to help her. She'd come here with the intent to gain an ally and she had. Still, she couldn't resist scanning the ballroom one more time for Inigo as her partner led her back to the sidelines, but he wasn't to be found. He'd already gone. She remembered that. He never stayed long at any party. Funny, how one could go five years without seeing someone, training oneself not to think about that person, then one encounter was all it took to break that carefully constructed dam and everything came flooding back. Audevere touched her gloved fingertips to her lips. *Everything.*

* * *

She dreamt that night of Collin, of all of them together that halcyon summer that had been filled with a young girl's every fantasy: her debut, her whirlwind engagement to a charming young man.

They were picnicking in the Richmond woods, having gone down the Thames on a barge. They were a rather large group as they strolled beneath the leafy canopy of the trees.

She slowed her pace, steadily falling behind the group and taking Inigo with her. She wanted to tease him; he was too serious by far.

'You were watching us,' she accused playfully when the group was out of earshot.

'I beg your pardon?' Boscastle's heir was all starch.

Audevere gave a merry laugh and twirled her parasol. She slanted him a coy look. That should have done the trick: the laugh, the look. 'You act as if I've accused you of high treason!' Many gentlemen in London found the combination irresistible, but not Inigo. He was not enchanted in the least. It only made her more determined to crack him.

'You've accused me of something nearly as bad. You make me out to be a voyeur, which many would call a rather sordid hobby.' He arched a slim, immaculate brow as she tapped him with her fan.

'A voyeur! La! You are a wicked man. Such dark thoughts lurking in your head. It's always the quiet ones,' she flirted. Any other young beau would have risen to the bait and argued the point teasingly. But from Inigo there was nothing.

She made an exasperated pout, a practised, pretty one she'd worked on in the mirror, one that took advantage of the fine shape of her mouth. 'Don't you ever smile?'

'When I have something to smile about,' he informed her with all seriousness.

'Collin smiles all the time.' Perhaps some friendly competition would spur him to engage more fully in the conversation—or at the very least he'd take the hint she'd so broadly implied and offer her the compliment for which she was fishing.

'His is a charmed life,' came the polite, oblique reply.

'Is yours not?' she probed with another coy glance meant to invite confidences.

'My life is quite satisfactory.' Another oblique, useless reply.

'Has anyone ever told you that you're a difficult conversationalist?' She slipped her free hand through his arm and felt him stiffen at her bold overture. 'Do I make you uncomfortable?'

'You should be walking up front with Collin.' He ignored her question altogether, the maddening man. It was all she could do not to stamp her foot, cross her arms, pout for real and demand his attention.

'I always walk with Collin. Besides, he is surrounded by admirers, as usual,' She gave an airy wave of her hand. If there was one thing she would have changed about today's picnic it would have been the number of revellers and more specifically the number of pretty, well-born girls.

'You needn't worry. Collin admires you the most,' Inigo offered.

'I would thank you for the reassurance, should I have needed it.' She adjusted her parasol, pretending he'd paid her a compliment.

'It's not reassurance; it's the truth. And you do need it, pardon my opinion. You worry all the time about whether or not you're good enough for him. I can tell you most assuredly that you aren't.'

He was right. She did worry. One day Collin would wake up and realise he could do better, that aside from her expensive gowns and her good looks, she was nothing, just the daughter of a merchant ship's captain. Inigo Vellanoweth had already seen it because he wasn't momentarily blinded by love. Audevere's temper rose; she hated being exposed and especially by this man who plainly did not care for her. 'Should I take my clothes off and dance naked in the grass? You seem to have stripped me bare.'

'I'd rather you not,' came his dry reply.

'Why don't you like me?' She persisted in confronting him. If she pushed him far enough, she could make him pay for that remark.

'It's not that I don't like you. It's that I don't like you for him. For Collin.'

'I don't think I've ever been so blatantly insulted twice in such a short amount of time. You have a rare gift,' Audevere snapped. Dear Lord, did this man never stop? Such unpleasantness beneath his austerely handsome face.

'I am sorry if you find honesty insulting.'

She chose to ignore the barb and swung the conversation back to his previous comment. 'Is that why you stare? I catch you at it all the time. Are you imagining who I might suit better?' He said nothing and she gave a sly smile, pressing on. 'You are imagining me with someone else. I'll take that as a challenge. Who might that someone be?' She scanned the group walking ahead of them. 'One of your friends? Lynford, maybe? Or...' her gaze swivelled back to him pointedly '...maybe the someone is you.' It was an outrageously shocking thought to voice, to accuse an honourable man of coveting his friend's fiancée. She knew she'd gone beyond the limits of propriety in her temper, but she wanted payback for his cutting remarks.

She tapped her fingers on his sleeve in feigned congeniality. 'Is it you? Do you fancy that you are man enough for me? Better than Collin? That's hardly a flattering thing to think about a friend. Are you sure you wouldn't be slumming?'

'Stop it! This conversation has gone far enough. You are speaking nonsense.' He disengaged her hand from his sleeve, her arm from his arm.

She smiled, widely, with laughter in her eyes on purpose. He wanted her to be ashamed. She would be anything but. 'Ha!' she wanted to say. 'I got a rise out of you, after all.' But Collin was cutting through the group, making his way to where they lingered in the rear.

'Ah, this is sweetness itself, my best friend and my future wife, chatting away, already friends.' Collin slipped his arms through theirs, putting himself in the middle. 'What scintillating things have you two been discussing back here while I've been missing all the fun?'

Audevere answered his smile with one of her own, deliberately sunny to prove a point. 'You, of course. Always you. I was telling Tintagel he should take his cue from you and smile more.'

Collin flashed her one of his dazzling grins. 'But, my dear, he can't possibly smile as much as I do; he hasn't as much as I have to be happy about. After all, I have you, the most beautiful girl of the Season— or any Season, if you ask me.' Collin brightened further, if that was possible. He tugged at her arm. 'Have you seen the strawberry patch in the glen? You must come, Aud.' He was already leading her away and she let him. She wondered if there really were any strawberries this late in the summer, or if it was merely an excuse to get her alone and steal kisses. She didn't mind. She liked Collin's kisses. Even if she hadn't, she would have let him kiss her anyway—anything to hold his attention. Her father would kill her if she lost Collin, second son of a duke. She wondered if she should ask her father to have the wedding moved up. A nine-month engagement suddenly seemed like an eternity. She couldn't lose him.

But she felt Inigo's eyes burning into her back as Collin led her away...

Audevere sat up in bed, her nightgown clinging to her body, sticky with sweat and remembrances. The past had bled into the present, despite her best efforts to wall it off, to forget those glorious months when she'd been one of them, accepted in the inner circle of the group known to London as the Cornish Dukes. She'd been innocent of much in those days, unaware of the full extent of her father's corruption. She'd been happy, her days filled with Collin's smile and Inigo's sharp sparring, her evenings spent dancing beneath glittering chandeliers in Collin's arms. But those weren't the dances that lingered in her mind now, nor the arms. She could hardly remember how Collin's arms felt. It was Inigo's waltz and Inigo's arms that haunted her now.

She shook her head. It was disloyal of her to forget Collin, to have his memory pushed aside by his friend. Maybe she was disloyal? She'd always denied this, but perhaps she was wrong. Her father's words rang in her ears. *'Blood will tell.'* Perhaps he and Inigo were right. Perhaps there was no good in her, after all.

Audevere was up to no good, he could sense it. Brenley tapped his fingers on the polished surface of his desk, thinking as the sun came up. It was his wont to start the day a step ahead of everyone else. He was seldom abed after dawn. In fact, he hadn't gone to bed since returning from the Bradford ball. His mind was too active, too suspicious. Audevere had been far too biddable. Everything had gone far too well. Last night, Tremblay had invited her to an equestrian exhibit at Prince Baklanov's riding school in Leicester Square. She'd done as he'd asked, making conspicuous efforts to win back Tremblay's attentions.

All this, after she'd voiced some reticence towards the match. He knew his daughter. She was stubborn like him. There was more to her caginess than he could presently identify. It had been too easy to persuade her to re-engage Tremblay's attentions. Perhaps he was supposed to believe she wanted to be a viscountess after all, or that his arguments were every bit as persuasive as they ought to be. Once, he might have believed those reasons easily. Once, she'd been a malleable young girl who'd done his bidding. She'd not questioned him when he'd told her to be nice to certain gentlemen invited to dinner; she'd not questioned him when he'd told her to break off the engagement to Collin Truscott, because she knew the consequences if she did not.

Was that fear enough now? He used fear as a tactic rather liberally. Blackmail was based on it. But fear had a shelf life, its potency short-lived. What if she no longer feared the secrets he held about her? Brenley rose and strode to the console to pour himself a drink, choosing to forget it was morning now and not night. He forced himself to think. Why would she no longer fear the airing of those secrets? Surely she understood Tremblay couldn't protect her from them? Did she think Inigo Vellanoweth could? Had that dance been about more than creating competition to motivate Tremblay? And there'd been those unexplained moments outside on the veranda. He'd not asked about those. If she was planning something, he didn't want to tip his hand and alert her.

He smiled into his drink. What did she think she could do to him? It was intriguing to think about. He owned her body and soul, just as he'd owned her mother. There was little she could do, but it would be interesting to watch her try. If that should allow him to bring down Inigo Vellanoweth in the process, all the better. That man had it coming to him after stealing the Blaxford mines from his control.

Brenley finished his drink and rang for two footmen, tall, skilled men he'd hired for more than their ability to look impressive in livery. 'I want the watch on Miss Brenley intensified,' he told them. 'I have reason to believe there might be an attempt to compromise her safety.' The men nodded. He went to his desk and pulled out two small bags of coins. 'Please keep a careful watch on her for me. I want to know where she goes and who she sees at all times. But, of course, I don't want her to know. It would unnerve her and cause her undue anxiety. I will expect full reports daily.' Now, he would wait and see what would come of this. He'd let out the leash on Aude-vere—but only allowed her just enough rope to see if she hung herself.

Chapter Five

'No good will come of this.' Vennor Penlerick, the blond, tousled, and too recently roused from sleep Duke of Newlyn, rubbed his temples over breakfast.

Inigo poured him a cup of coffee and mixed in a generous splash of whisky. 'Late night?' he commiserated, handing Vennor the steaming cup. Ever since Vennor's father had died it seemed it was always a late night for Vennor.

Vennor grunted something that approximated 'thank you' and cracked open an eye. 'Not for the reasons you think.'

So, he could cross that hypothesis off his list, that Vennor had been out getting bosky. 'A woman, then? Is she still upstairs?' Inigo pressed. He'd thought to see Vennor at the Bradford ball, but his friend had been conspicuously absent. At this point in the year, London was empty. It wasn't like during the Season where an eligible bachelor had four or five balls a night to choose from. Bradford's was the only place to be, but Vennor had declined to show.

Vennor grimaced his disapproval both at the idea and the fact that Inigo had suggested it. 'If it were, I'd never bring her here. You know me better than that.'

'Do I?' Inigo sat back in his chair, hands steepled contemplatively. It seemed these days he hardly knew Vennor at all. 'You've changed. You weren't at the Bradfords' last night.'

'That doesn't mean I've changed. It means I chose not to attend.'

'You've gone nowhere since Marianne Treleven went home. Or at least, nowhere that *I* know of.' Which meant nowhere decent—balls, autumn musicales, card parties with those few MPs still in town on government business.

Vennor brushed back a swoop of unruly golden hair that had fallen in his face and swallowed his coffee. 'Much to my regret, if the result is that you've taken up with the Brenleys.'

'Much to *my* regret,' Inigo countered, 'You are never where you are supposed to be these days.' He met his friend with a steely, cool gaze. 'Where are you spending your time?'

'No, you do not get to show up at my breakfast table, roust me from bed, drop the news that you're helping Audevere Brenley run away from home and then interrogate *me*. If anyone needs interrogating, it's you. Have you lost your mind? How do you know this isn't a double cross, that her father put her up to it to expose your hand? Or to trap you into a marriage with his daughter?'

'Because I asked her last night. I had those same thoughts as well.'

Vennor snorted. 'Let me guess—she denied them. And you believed her?'

'She does not wish to be her father's pawn any longer. He will continue to use her until he marries her off and perhaps even beyond that.' If she stayed, it wouldn't end, ever. As he explained it to Vennor now, he saw more clearly the desperation that drove her rather rash decision.

Vennor arched a doubting blond brow. 'His pawn? Are you sure she didn't mean his accomplice?' Inigo would have been more upset at Vennor's cynicism if it hadn't so closely mirrored his own at one time. But Vennor could be forgiven. He hadn't seen the fear in her eyes, or heard the desperation in her voice that she had tried so hard to hide.

'Why now? Why hasn't she come forward sooner?' Vennor pressed.

'Collin's death was an epiphany for her,' Inigo explained patiently, using her own arguments from the night before. 'His death made her aware of the full extent of her father's corruption and its consequences.'

'So aware and so conflicted that she's waited five years to run away?' Vennor didn't try to hide his disbelief. Sarcasm dripped from his tongue.

'She admits to being something of an ostrich with

her head in the sand, trying to believe it wouldn't happen again, helped along by mourning Collin and then the mine scandal. Those events bought her some time off the Marriage Mart. And in truth, Vennor, what was she to do? What power did she have? Where could she have gone?'

'And she's chosen you to help her, a man who is willing to do her bidding and even make excuses for her. How convenient. I am sorry, but it smacks of a set-up, dear friend. I would be doing you a disservice not to say it. She is manipulating you.'

'It isn't like that. There were intangibles, you didn't see her, hear her.' How could he explain to Vennor what he had felt in her presence?

Vennor chuckled. 'Intangibles? I am sure there were. Moonlight, a pretty girl in a pretty dress. A very compelling setting indeed. Men have died for such things before. I just never imagined you'd be one of them.'

Vennor speared him with a look of smug victory. 'Yes, I said it. Perhaps Brenley has decided he's done with you. He wants to end whatever threat you may pose to him with your information and he wants revenge for the Blaxford mines. He already had a hand in leading Collin to his death and a hand in attempting Eliza's death last year. Why not yours? He won't go after your money or your reputation; they are both unassailable. He'll go after you, though. You are flesh and blood like any other man.'

'I see you're awake now,' Inigo commented slyly. Vennor's capable mind was running at full speed now.

Vennor finished off the coffee and poured another cup, his toast untouched. 'I am always awake, these days.' Inigo thought that was probably true. Vennor had the look of a man who didn't sleep: dark circles, hollows at his cheeks. 'Promise me you'll be careful? Promise me you'll ask for help if you need it?' Vennor encouraged. He pushed back from the table. 'Now that's settled and, since you're here, shall we fence? I need a good sparring partner.' He gestured for a footman to bring the fencing gear to the ballroom.

Inigo rose with him and the two friends made their way to the enormous, empty ballroom of Newlyn House. 'I hear you pinked Sedgwick at Jackson's the other day.' Young Sedgwick had sold his mother's jewels to cover gambling debts. It had been a very public, very shameful incident since he'd had to steal them first out of his mother's jewel box.

'Sedgwick was careless.' Vennor shrugged off the mention. 'He'll not make that mistake again.' Inigo thought there were other mistakes Sedgwick would not make again, too. But that was Vennor: a subtle advocate for family and justice wherever and however that advocacy was needed.

They put on their masks and selected their rapiers. Inigo tested his with an experimental slash. 'This set is new. It has good balance.'

'They're from Leodegrance's fencing salon in

Paris,' Vennor offered, taking up his position in the centre of the floor and signalling his readiness. *'En garde.'* Vennor opened, launching his offensive, attempting to attack high inside, but Inigo was ready for him.

'You are very predictable today.' Inigo parried.

'Unlike falling in love, you'll have to watch yourself with Audevere.' Vennor lunged. So much for anything being settled.

'Love is not the issue here. This is about helping a woman in distress,' Inigo insisted with a sharp riposte. 'This is all business and chivalry.'

What had Audevere said in the moonlight? *'Because Collin would have wanted you to help me... because once you liked me just a little.'* Those had been potent words, words he'd not shared with Vennor. He made another sharp parry. 'Besides, I am not looking to marry.'

Vennor gave a harsh laugh. 'Neither were Cassian and Eaton. Now look at them. Eaton has an instant family and Cassian has abandoned us to traipse around Europe for a year on honeymoon.'

'I'm not Eaton or Cassian,' Inigo said drily. He did, however, see the irony in it. Of the four of them, only Vennor was expected to marry sooner instead of later, the only son of the late Richard Penlerick and the new Duke of Newlyn. Should his bough on the family tree break without a son to inherit, the dukedom would pass out of the Penlerick family to a rather distant relative who didn't necessarily share the code of the Cornish Dukes.

'The point is, Eaton and Cassian didn't expect it, but it found them anyway. Love is rather like lightning. We don't know when it will strike, where or whom. I'd rather not see it strike you anywhere near Audevere Brenley.'

Inigo felt a stab of defensiveness on her behalf. He feinted to the right and nearly got away with a surprise attack to Vennor's left shoulder, but Vennor had got faster.

'I appreciate your concern.' Inigo grunted, concentrating on the blades.

'She's a canny girl and the distressed damsel is an intoxicating one for honourable males such as ourselves.'

'She's scared,' Inigo countered. 'She knows there are consequences to leaving. I think she's very brave.' This time, Inigo got his tip high on Vennor's shoulder. 'First point to me.'

'And the last one you'll earn.' Vennor growled, disappointed in himself. They reset to begin again, Inigo taking the offensive.

'How ironic she comes to you,' Vennor mused. Their thin blades clicked against each other in fast succession as Inigo pushed him to give up ground. 'You were the only one who could resist her flirting.'

The comment caught him, guilt pricking. Vennor had it wrong. He'd been the one to lust after her, while the others had merely been charmed. He'd actually indulged in the fantasy of imagining her as his. 'Ha!' Vennor's blade slipped inside his guard. 'You weren't concentrating.'

'No, I wasn't,' Inigo conceded. He was too distracted to be a fair opponent today. Vennor would see that distraction and wonder about it. He put up his blade. 'We must call it a draw this morning. I need to make some calls before the day is too advanced.'

Vennor raised an eyebrow in question. 'You're already jumping to do her bidding. What does she have you doing?'

Inigo stripped off his mask 'She's asked for nothing yet. Just that I wait.' He'd never been very good at playing the passive role. He'd far rather have a task to carry out, something he could do to assist her. He did not like to sit idly by.

He was still waiting four days later, sitting at White's and enjoying a brandy as he read the newspapers, which were less enjoyable and more worrisome than his brandy. The society columns reported Tremblay was dancing attendance on Audevere once more—or was it that she was dancing attendance on Tremblay, as one astute columnist pointed out. He was in two minds about that. Of course she would be pursuing the connection in order to appease her father. She couldn't quit Tremblay cold without arousing suspicion. On the other hand, was it possible she'd changed her mind? Was it possible she'd thought about his argument that perhaps Tremblay's title would be enough to protect her without the need to give up life as she knew it? Maybe that would be best; it would put her out his purview for good.

His gut disagreed that was the case, though. She'd been in earnest that night on the veranda. Likewise, if she'd meant to draw Inigo into her father's web for some nefarious purpose, that, too, seemed unlikely since she'd made no further overture. It was hard to draw someone in if there was no contact. Perhaps she was having difficulty getting word to him? Without the activity of the Season throwing people together on a daily basis, it wasn't easy for unmarried men and women of good birth to meet without risking speculation and scandal. Darker thoughts encroached on that idea. Was she in danger? Had her father not believed her explanation for dancing with him? Did he dare go to Brenley's town house and ask to see her?

That would be action at least. In the waiting, he'd at last put his finger on what niggled at him. Waiting was reactive. Audevere running away was reactive. Yes, leaving had the potential to put her beyond Brenley's reach, but it only put *her* beyond Brenley's reach. It didn't stop Brenley; it only stripped him of one of his tools. She would run and Brenley would continue as he always had, using others for his personal gain and turning a blind eye to the consequences. But perhaps the loss of his daughter would weaken him, then Inigo could strike with the evidence he had gathered against Brenley.

A footman approached, bowing as he held out a salver containing a single folded note. Inigo took the paper, trying not to get his hopes up. It was not an uncommon occurrence for notes to find him here. There was always word of this investment, that cargo, or rates on the Exchange. But this was not one of those notes. His business partners did not address him as *My dear Inigo.*

He could hear the throaty seduction of her voice as he read the words. At last, Audevere had sent word—six of them to be precise.

A ripple of tension moved through him as his eyes scanned down the page. The message was simple:

Play cards at the Thurstons' tonight.

She was ready to act. The summons implied as much. But she'd been careful to omit what those actions were, testament to a need for secrecy and perhaps her difficulty in getting word to him. Nevertheless, he was far too clever to accept the implication of action at face value. In his experience, implications spawned more implications.

Inigo refolded the note and tapped his fingers against his thigh, restless energy coursing through him. Vennor's doubts, which were echoes of his own lingering ones, kept him cautious, kept his energy on a tight leash. The rather short notice did not escape him. The Thurstons' card party was just a few hours away. Should he answer the summons? He didn't

deny there was a certain thrill at the thought of seeing her again and that thrill wanted him to accept
with alacrity, to run headlong to her side after four
days of cooling his heels. But caution's leash reined
him in. He could not afford to rush in blindly, no
matter how much he wanted to believe her protesta-
tions of innocence. He *would* go, but on his terms.
She had made him wait and now he would return the
favour. She had to be made to understand that she
was not the puppet master in this scenario, no matter how beautiful she was.

Six hours later, as the hall clock in the hall of
Thurston House struck nine, Inigo stood in the doorway of the drawing room, his eyes quartering the
tables of card players until he found her seated near
the marble fireplace, her back to the door as she
raked in a trick, her laughter carried to him on the
waves of conversations. Even when facing a crisis,
she gave the appearance of being entirely at ease. It
brought a smile to his face to see her so untroubled,
not anxious as she had been at the Bradfords'. Perhaps he was part of the reason for her ease tonight.
Perhaps it was because she knew she wasn't alone,
that he was with her. It made him glad he'd come.

He lingered in the doorway, drinking her in: the
sound of her, that smoky, confident laugh; the sight
of her—her gold hair done up high, exposing her
long neck, the delicate puffed sleeves of her gown,
the scoop of her neckline. Her gown tonight was

reminiscent of a starry sky, a hazy twilight blue that bled into darker indigo hues at the hem where her skirts pooled about her chair. Desire stirred in him hard, the desire for the right to walk over to her, to lay his hand at the base of her delicate neck, to rub his thumb gently across the exposed skin in a gesture of idle, absent possession.

No, not possession, he corrected. She would not want to be possessed. She'd already been possessed by her father. A partnership then, he amended. It would be a gesture of togetherness, a gesture that said, we belong together. *We.*

It was a fantasy more dangerous than revenge. Her partner at the table rose and suddenly Inigo was in motion, moving across the room, ready to take his place.

Chapter Six

Audevere raked in the last trick of the hand, her pleasure over the win dimmed by Inigo's absence. What good was the card party if she could not use it as an excuse to meet him? It was nine o'clock and he wasn't here yet. It raised all nature of doubts. Had the note reached him? Or had he chosen to believe the worst of her and decided not to help her, after all? 'Well played, Miss Brenley,' her partner applauded. The young man, a nephew of the Thurstons, rose and stretched, his gaze moving towards a certain young lady at the pianoforte. 'Would any of you mind if I took a break?' he asked the table at large.

Good heavens, the boy was green! Audevere bit her lip to keep from laughing at his expense. Had no one warned him about their opponents? Mrs Whitfield and Major Banken, inveterate card players both, looked daggers at him for the suggestion and he sank back into his chair reluctantly.

'I am happy to sit in, if no one minds.' The tenor

tone raised the hairs of awareness on the back of her neck and ran goose pimples up her arms. Inigo was here. He had come. She pressed a hand to the reticule at her side, relief swamping her with a smile she didn't try to hide.

Thurston's nephew was eager to vacate his seat and introductions were quickly made. 'Tintagel, what a pleasure to see you. It's been a while.' Major Banken shook hands with him as he took the empty chair while Mrs Whitfield eyed him with frank appreciation. Young, handsome, rich, titled. Just her sort, the widow's bold eyes said as she dealt the next hand. She gave Audevere a warning smile, the sort one woman gives another when she wants to signal first rights to a man. But Audevere answered with a smile of her own. *Mine.*

Inigo Vellanoweth was hers. She let the thought settle as she organised her hand. He'd come for her. More importantly, he'd come because she'd asked. Her trust in him had not been misplaced. He would help her escape and become someone new. Someone better. Across the table, he held her gaze briefly, but it was long enough to take the smile from Mrs Whitfield's face and to heat her own, long enough to make her wonder if those were the only reasons he'd come. He was handsomely, if austerely, turned out. His dark hair was cut short in the back, longer in the front where it was brushed forward. Where other men wore coloured coats for the evening, he wore his usual black. His only concession to colour was the sapphire tie clip that winked in the folds of his white cravat and drew a woman's eye up to the sharp planes of his face and those haunting blue eyes.

They won the bid after three rounds of heated bidding, much to Mrs Whitfield's overt chagrin and the table fell quiet as play ensued. Inigo was an adept card player, reading her plays with astute accuracy, but they had to be careful. It was entirely possible they were over bid. They needed the next two tricks. Audevere played high, the ten of hearts, even though Inigo claimed the trick with his king. Would he catch the signal? Inigo's pale gaze caught hers, a lingering heat spreading low in her belly as he led out a low spade. Cards had never been sexier. Her breath was coming quick with excitement as she trumped and led out her remaining diamond for the win, Inigo favouring her with a rare, melting smile.

'Early luck,' Mrs Whitfield snorted in defeat.

'Care to try again?' Inigo grinned, neither of them missing the widow's innuendo. He was intoxicating like this, Audevere realised. Here at the card table, she had his trust completely. If this was a fleeting glimpse of what having his trust felt like, possessing it entirely would be a wondrous thing. It would be a lucky woman indeed who would capture that. The woman would not be her, though. She would be gone soon and he would be lost to her, along with the rest of this world. Best to enjoy the moment, she scolded herself, and not worry over what could never be. Inigo gave a gentle cough, reminding her it was her turn to bid. She passed.

They played the second hand on defence, keeping Mrs Whitfield and the Major from making their bid. Inigo smiled his silent approval as the Major dealt the last hand. What would it be like to transfer this mutual confidence in one another from the card table to real life, if only for the duration of their partnership? If she could not fantasise about the future, surely she could entertain fantasies for the short term? But it was an equally dangerous thought and a more potent one. This was not the time to be drawn to someone, not now when she was looking to unmake her life and start a new one. Yet the appeal of Inigo was undeniable.

Her mind whispered rationales which were meant to be comforting: *It is only because he is helping you, because he reminds you of better days. It is natural you feel that way.*

She looked down into her hand and waited for Inigo to bid. The tea trolley rolled in, signalling this would be the last hand. Inigo exchanged a look with her; soon they'd have time to talk alone.

Perhaps that sense of exigence drove him as well as her. Inigo upped the bid in abrupt fashion, making it impossible for the Major to outbid him, and then proceeded to play the hand at a commanding pace, never once giving up the lead until the last trick was claimed.

'Nicely done,' the Major commended, all of them

a bit breathless at the speed and excitement Inigo's play had generated. But there'd been no stopping Inigo, no slowing him down.

'I could see what I wanted and I went for it,' Inigo commented, flashing her a glance that made her think the remark had little to do with the cards. He nodded to her and rose. 'Miss Brenley, you were an outstanding partner. Might I offer you a turn about the room?' And quite possibly out of doors, his pale-blue eyes said.

'Nothing would delight me more.' She smiled as she laid her hand on his dark sleeve.

'You came,' she said in low tones when they were out of earshot of the table. 'I was beginning to worry you might not.' As relieved as she was to see him, he needed to understand the worry he'd caused her.

'You gave me very short notice,' he replied point-edly, not liking her scold. Ah, so his late arrival was a lesson of sorts. She took note. Inigo was an hon-ourable man, a loyal man, but not a pliable man. It was a reminder that while she knew him, there was also much of him she did not know.

They stopped before a Constable landscape, pre-tending to study it. 'I had little choice,' she explained in soft tones. 'It is difficult to get word to you and my opportunities to meet you are limited. I am watched constantly.' She could understand his position, but he must also understand the gravity of hers.

He slanted her a doubting glance, the trust of the

card table in question here. 'And this evening? Are you not also watched tonight?'

'In a way. The coachman would report any stops I made, but here inside, my father's servants cannot follow me. For a few hours at a social event I might be a little freer, but not entirely. Our hostess has promised to keep an eye on me and my maid is in the kitchen with the other servants. Not that Lady Thurston would see strolling with you as a threat worthy of reporting to my father. Then there are the society columns which report who I am with, if they notice. Still, I cannot control who is also invited and there's always a chance the columns won't pay attention to a lowly card party in the middle of October.'

'Do you always think this way?' Inigo murmured, his sharp gaze tinged with sadness.

'Like a chess game? Yes. It comes with the territory. One cannot be Gismond Brenley's daughter and survive otherwise.' She gave a rueful shrug against the sadness in his gaze. She did not want his pity. 'No matter, that is all almost done with and I shall have a better life soon, one where I needn't think like a chess master.' She tried for a smile. 'Might we take the air for a moment?'

Inigo ushered her outside, through French doors to the balcony. He understood the need. Outdoors they could be alone and they could conduct the business that had drawn them here. He wished it was more than business that compelled them outdoors. He'd enjoyed playing cards and watching her smile across the table at him. She'd been intoxicating in her victories. What a pair they'd made, leading, trumping, bidding. He wanted more of that, more of smiling Audevere, less of this…business.

On the balcony, she loosened the strings of her reticule. 'I wanted to give you these tonight. Hold out your hands.'

He cupped his hands and she poured a small pile of jewellery into them: a strand of pearls, tiny diamond earrings, some diamond-tipped hairpins and an old-fashioned brooch studded with sapphires around a cameo. 'It's not much,' she apologised when he said nothing. 'I want you to pawn them for me, turn them into cash.'

'These are yours?' The import was not lost on him. This was the next step in her departure. Before she could run away, she had to have funds.

'Yes. The ones I have access to, at least. My father keeps the other jewels locked in the safe.' She bit her lip, her fear from the Bradford ball reasserting itself. 'I could not get to them without him knowing.'

'Will he not miss these if you don't wear them?' She needed to understand that pawning them put the plan into irrevocable motion. She would need to leave soon, before the missing jewels aroused suspicion.

'Not before I'm gone,' she replied staunchly, her eyes meeting his in understanding, and her bravery touched a small piece of his heart, a piece he tried to keep locked away for fear it made him vulnerable. Caring for Audevere Brenley had been hurtful business in the past. He wasn't eager to hurt again, but perhaps it was too late for that.

Inigo thumbed the brooch. 'And this piece? It's not like the rest.' It was for an older woman, not a young girl.

'It was my mother's.' The admission came softly, almost shyly. No one ever spoke of Lady Brenley and he sensed her reticence to elaborate. It was one more piece of the Brenley mystery. Gismond's wife had been dead before Gismond had come to London, his lovely daughter in tow. 'I'm not sure my father even knows I have it,' she confessed.

Or it might not have been allowed, Inigo thought. But the piece meant something to her. 'Are you sure you want to sell it?'

'I don't have a choice.' Audevere's gaze drifted out over the dark gardens. For too much of her life she'd had no choice. It was not the first time he'd heard her use that phrase and he was tired of it on her behalf.

'There's always a choice, Aud.' The old nickname slipped between them before he could call it back.

She turned her gaze to him, her eyes soft with memories. 'No one's called me that for a long time.' Not since Collin died, he'd wager. Damn, but the night was becoming intimate, full of confidences and secrets. For a moment her body swayed towards him and he imagined she wanted more from him than a saviour to whisk her away. He was tempted to gather her to him, to kiss away her fears, her regrets, her belief that she had no choice. Instead, he took the brooch and pressed it into her hand, curling her fingers around it.

'Keep it. I will give you the money if it comes to it,' he said, his voice rough with emotion.

'No.' Her answer was swift and sure, a bolt that shattered the intimacy of the night and reminded him, perhaps reminded them both, that what lay between them was business. She gave it back to him. 'I will not take money from you. Too many men have given me gifts, much to my detriment. I did not ask for your money. I could never repay it.'

'I do not ask for repayment,' Inigo argued. His mind was already running through options, already taking her plans from her and making them his own. Where could he settle her? Where could he find her property? Where could he set up an account for her? He could keep her safe and in comfort. He needn't lose her when she gave up this world and she needn't be abandoned... But that wasn't the kind of help she'd come seeking.

'Then the money will be between us for ever, a debt that will hang over me. I want no debts.' She wanted no one to have leverage over her, that was what she meant. Inigo saw that clearly. Men like Gismond Brenley did most of their business that way, holding secrets and debts over other men in order to get what they wanted. It made him wonder what leverage Brenley had over his own daughter. What experiences had taught her to be wary of gifts? Even those given in friendship? It was just one more piece of the mystery of her, proof that the Audevere Brenley he'd once known was only a small part of who she was. For such old acquaintances, they knew very little of one another.

'All right,' he conceded, slipping the jewels into his jacket pocket. A woman had her pride as much as any man and Audevere's pride had been strained. 'I will arrange to sell them. Give me three days.'

'We can meet at the Tetford musicale,' she offered, all business again. He wanted the other Audevere back, the one who had blushed when he'd looked at her tonight, the one who'd coolly answered Mrs Whitfield's coy smile with one of her own. He'd liked what he'd read in that smile. *Mine.* If only for tonight, if only for a little while. Did she feel it, too? This pull that tempted, that had nothing to do with the business of escaping? The pull that would be there regardless?

'And then we must discuss leaving,' Inigo offered gently, not wanting to break the spell, but knowing time alone was at a premium. 'It can be simple. I can have a carriage ready any time you want. We can merely drive away. But we need to have a place to go, we need to be able to leave undetected. I want as much time as possible between our departure and your father's discovery of your absence and that requires a plan. Will you let me make one, at least?' He would have to give her up. They needed to return to the party for propriety's sake and for his. If he stayed out here with her, he might be tempted to take a taste of what could never be.

'Thank you,' she murmured, stalling him when he would have led them indoors. 'You've been very good to me, Inigo.' She moved against him then, her arms going about his neck in an unmistakable gesture. She meant to kiss him, and he was about to allow it, except for one thing: her remark about gifts.

Inigo put his hands at her waist and set her apart. 'What are you doing, Aud?' he asked gently.

'I think you know very well what I'm doing.' Her eyes danced a little as she teased him, perhaps disguising her hurt with playfulness. 'I've kissed you before.'

'A parlour game, nothing more,' he reminded her. 'We're not playing games now, Aud. You are not required to kiss me in return for my assistance.'

She lowered her gaze, her cheeks flushing a bit at the gentle scold. 'Isn't that what damsels in distress offer their knights in shining armour? Surely such chivalry deserves a reward?'

A dark suspicion was beginning to take specific form about the sort of lessons she'd learned about men bearing gifts and anger formed with it, anger at Gismond Brenley who'd allowed his daughter to learn such a thing. What sort of father permitted men to make advances more suited to mistresses and high-priced whores? He tipped her chin up, forcing her to look at him. 'Damsels only kiss their knights if they want to.'

'Maybe,' Audevere whispered, 'this damsel wants to. Maybe I've been wanting to kiss you all night, ever since you led that spade and let me trump us to victory.' If only this were London in Season, if only things were different between them, then he might allow this piece of flirtation.

'Aud, we don't want to do this.' No matter that his body argued quite eloquently to the contrary. He did want to kiss her; his attraction to her was undeniable, a palpable thing he could feel when they were together. This was something else entirely separate from kisses for services rendered, something heady, intoxicating, with a life of its own and he could absolutely not allow it to happen. Not when she felt she owed him something, not when there was much he'd not yet settled for himself in regards to Audevere and his own feelings. He could not tarnish her with his guilt. If he ever kissed her, he wanted it to be pure, and without ulterior motive.

If?

Or did he mean *when*?

'Let's go inside. I don't want you to catch cold.' Not that there was any chance of that. They were both burning.

Chapter Seven

Her cheeks were still burning three days later at the Tetford musicale, at least metaphorically, every time she thought of her silliness on the balcony at the Thurstons'. Audevere smoothed her skirts and stepped into the drawing room, her maid already disposed of downstairs. She hoped to have arrived before Inigo. She could use a moment or two to compose herself before facing him. She'd had three days to process her foolishness. She understood now that she'd been swept away by the moment, by the evening, by his kindnesses. She'd mistaken that kindness for something else, perhaps misread him entirely, taken his liking for something more, fuelled by remembering the parlour-game kiss as something more than a game.

She had only herself to blame and she understood that, too. She'd been caught up in the emotional tangle of recent events. It wasn't every day a girl decided to disappear and reinvent herself all on her own. Life was suddenly more overwhelming than it usually was and she'd been overcome by it in a moment of weakness. She would explain it all to Inigo tonight when she saw him and they could go on as they had been before: old acquaintances trading on a fragile new friendship that was meant to be short-lived.

It might even be the shortest friendship she'd had, if one considered last week as the beginning of it and next week the end of it. *Next week*. A bolt of reality hit her in the stomach like a punch. This time next week she would not be in a drawing room, wearing silk gowns, surrounded by elegant people. Nor the week after that, or perhaps ever. This was all going to end. Soon. No exact day of departure had been determined, but it wouldn't be later than next week; it couldn't be. Events were in motion that demanded she not delay.

'There you are, my dear.' Kindly Mrs Tetford found her in the crowd and linked her arm through hers. 'I'm so glad you could come tonight.' Mrs Tetford had offered to act as her chaperon and Audevere was glad for the chance to escape the watchful eyes her father had at home. 'Tremblay is here, of course. I imagine you'll want to see him and his friend Tintagel is here as well. They seem to be a pair this autumn. Perhaps they've discovered they have you in common, my dear. I've never had such esteemed company at my musicale.' Mrs Tetford patted her arm knowingly and chattered away, oblivious to Audevere's reaction. Inigo was here already.

'I would like to see the Viscount.' Audevere smiled at her hostess. If he was smart, he'd be with Tremblay and Inigo was nothing if not socially astute. He'd understand the most direct, least conspicuous way to meet her here would be to stay close to Tremblay.

She was not disappointed. They were no more than halfway across the room when she sighted Inigo standing beside the Viscount, the two men engaged in an animated conversation. Then Inigo spotted her and his attention changed, his gaze riveting on her progress as if she were the only woman in the room. It was enough to bring the heat back to her cheeks and to make her doubt her silliness. Perhaps what had driven her to that spontaneous, rejected kiss had not been imagined after all. Perhaps he had not rejected her efforts because he was without feeling, but because he felt too much? How could a man look at her that way and feel nothing?

'Miss Brenley, charmed as always.' Tremblay bent over her hand.

'And as always, I am honoured.' Audevere made a little dip of a curtsy and favoured him with a smile. Anyone watching them would expect it. They'd been a most studied couple this Season. She needed to play the part. The last thing she wanted right now was to present anyone with anything out of the ordinary which might be, even unintentionally, reported to her father.

She turned to Inigo. 'How nice to see you, Lord

Tintagel.' How did one manage from here? People were beginning to take their seats. The performance would start soon and then she wouldn't have a chance to be alone with Inigo until intermission. She needn't have worried. Inigo had arranged even this small detail.

'Lord Tremblay and I have seats in the back with his sister if you would care to join us?' Inigo offered. 'His sister is sitting there now.' He gestured to a set of chairs near the French doors where a blonde woman sat, chatting with other matrons.

Acceptance was a matter of course, but Audevere marvelled at how smoothly it had all been arranged, how naturally it all flowed. She hated to use Tremblay and his sister as decoys, but it was surely better than trapping the man in marriage.

'I hear the soprano is mesmerising. We can slip out once the performance starts and no one will be the wiser.' It was only to conduct business, she told herself, but the whisper of his voice and the touch of his hand at her back didn't stop her pulse from racing, or her mind from wanting to pretend the assignation was for more personal reasons. More silliness, she scolded herself. No matter what she thought she saw in his eyes, she'd do best to keep herself under control or else risk her escape altogether. Inigo would be wary of helping a woman who threw herself at his head.

They took their seats and Audevere exchanged small talk with Tremblay's sister who was quite keen to make her acquaintance. She apparently had not been informed there would be no offer forthcoming from her brother. Inigo sat beside her, his very nearness causing her body to hum with an awareness that made it difficult to concentrate on anything else. Fortunately, they didn't have to wait long. The soprano began promptly at eight, a beautiful Italian woman with long dark hair, luminous eyes and an equally beautiful voice. Twenty minutes into the performance, Inigo quietly excused himself. Five minutes later, Audevere followed him into the gardens.

The Tetford gardens had not been shut down for autumn. The trickle of a fountain murmured at the heart of the garden and she followed the sound, finding Inigo sitting on the fountain's edge and looking entirely at ease, as if he invited women into dark gardens all the time. Perhaps he did. It was an interesting question. He was handsome enough for a woman to follow him anywhere without much cajolery. It was time to put aside such thoughts, though.

'Were you able to sell the jewellery?' she asked as he looked up from the fountain's basin.

'Yes.' His eyes held hers. 'It was a decent sum. It will help cover expenses for food and clothes, when you get to where you want to go.' He was discreetly asking her for details she didn't have. Yet. He reached into his coat and pulled out a leather bag and handed it to her. It was satisfyingly heavy, but she knew that heaviness to be an illusion. Every time she reached into the bag, she would be lessening its weight with no guarantee of being able to refill it. How would she support herself in her new life? The enormity of what she intended to do swamped her again. This bag was all that stood between her and starvation and homelessness. Well, not quite *all* that stood between her and defeat. There was Inigo, too, and his honour.

'Thank you.' She tucked the bag inside her reticule. It weighed just enough to be believable. Inigo had not augmented it with extra coin. She'd feared he would try. But he'd understood she was serious about making her own way. She smiled, hoping he'd divine the entirety of the reasons for her thanks. She pulled the purse strings tight.

'Will you allow me to make arrangements?' Inigo offered once more as he had at the Thurstons'. This time, she was tempted to give in. He'd given her time and she had no more plan than she'd had three days ago. He took her silence as a sign of permission. 'I can arrange for a cottage in Devonshire, on the Cornish border. Devonshire is wild, unpopulated. You would pass unnoticed, undiscovered.'

The generous offer touched her, tempted her, even as it stirred her wariness. Did he think she wouldn't see what he intended? 'And if I were discovered, you'd be on hand to ride to my rescue,' she put in pointedly. 'I seem to recall the Boscastle family seat is not far from that border. I could easily take refuge there if need be.' She shook her head. 'I will not have you set me up. Someone would be sure to notice the connection eventually. I mean to cut all ties. It would be too easy to have someone discover me through you.' She softened her refusal. 'I appreciate the offer, but you're already in enough danger just for helping me. If my father suspects you assisted me, you will likely be the first place he comes for answers.'

'I would welcome it,' Inigo offered fiercely and she was reminded that he'd once complained he couldn't publicly claim revenge through helping her. The man seated beside her, for all his smooth manners and urbane good looks, harboured a warrior inside. 'Although he will probably think twice. Anyone who takes on me, takes on the Cornish Dukes as well. He will not seek that confrontation.'

How nice to feel so invincible, Audevere thought. But also how misleading. Everyone had a chink in their armour. Her father had taught her that—a valuable lesson, if cruelly learned. 'Inigo, he can get to anyone,' she tried to caution him.

'Not this time. Listen. I have been gathering evidence over the last several years and I finally have enough to petition the King to strip him of his title. Will you allow me to make that petition known to your father?'

She took a moment to process what he was telling her, the power of it causing hope to blossom. 'You mean to use it as leverage against him, to prevent him from acting dishonestly again,' she surmised. 'He may keep his title as long as he refrains from abusing his position and you will be there to ensure that he doesn't.' It was genius to take a page from her father's book of tricks and leverage him instead. But it was also too dangerous. 'He would never allow such a thing to stand.'

'He could do nothing about it,' Inigo protested. 'The King may enjoy the money your father's endeavours bring to the royal coffers, but he will not want money with so much scandal attached to it, nor the disfavour of the Cornish Dukes. If the King has to choose where to confer favour—the Cornish Dukes or Sir Gismond Brenley—your father knows what his choice will be. In one move I can avenge Collin and give you your freedom. You needn't spend your life looking over your shoulder, fleeing at the slightest suspicion of discovery. You could take the Devonshire cottage, Aud, and be settled, perhaps not even give up your name.'

In that moment, with the moon overhead, the fountain trickling peacefully beside them, his eyes on her so trusting in the belief that every word he spoke was the truth, she felt her heart surge, felt it fill with emotion. He truly believed he could achieve all this with a piece of paper and she wanted to believe it was true, too, wanted to forget there were other secrets she was keeping, other secrets she *had* to keep for the well-being of anyone who sought to get too close to her. 'I can't take the cottage. It wouldn't be right even if it were possible.' How long would it be before one or both of them felt she owed him? How long would it be before her father discovered her and wielded her secret against Inigo's petition to the King?

'I ask for nothing in return, Aud.' He furrowed his brow and she watched the awful thought come to him as he remembered all she'd hinted at regarding men and favours. 'You don't think I'm setting you up to be my mistress, do you?' His affront was obvious; his cool eyes blazed. 'I would not dishonour Collin's memory by treating the woman he loved in such a manner.'

Collin? Was that why he hadn't kissed her? She'd found the only honourable man in England, a man who wanted her, but wouldn't act on it out of respect for a dead friend. She'd found quite the man to be her champion and it frustrated her even as it piqued her curiosity and caused her stomach to flutter.

She shouldn't have touched him, not after last time, but her hand acted on its own, sweeping his jaw with gentle fingers where dark stubble was starting to sprout. 'It's not just the cottage, Inigo. It's all your plan. It will never stand. Paper can't stop a bullet or a sword. He will send his men and they will do the dirty work for him in an alleyway.'

'They would have their work cut out for them,' he growled. She nodded. She'd seen him fence with Collin and there'd been shooting matches on summer picnics. He was skilled with both. But it wouldn't matter. Her father would never allow the odds to be even or fair.

What a rarefied world Inigo must live in to assume people would play by the rules. She would love him for it, if she could afford to. 'There's no point in debating it. We haven't much time left and you won't change my mind tonight. There are other things we must decide,' she added swiftly when he made to protest. She didn't want to hear his arguments for fear she might start to believe them.

What if she *could* believe them? What if she could have it all—her freedom, her father tethered? What sweet relief that would be, to think that scenario would allow her to keep Inigo, too, a constant champion, ready to ride to her rescue. *For Collin's sake*, the reminder whispered. He'd made that plain tonight. He'd not kissed her for Collin's sake and he was helping her for Collin's sake. Not for hers. Not for his own and not because *he* wanted to, but because he felt obliged to the memory of his dead friend.

'When shall we leave?' she asked, abruptly bringing them back to business.

Inigo blew out a breath, perhaps as frustrated as she. 'I am working on something with Tremblay to get your father out of town. Can you manage three more days?' he asked.

She drew a breath. 'Yes.' Three days. A lifetime of waiting and yet not much time at all to assemble what she needed and walk away from all she knew.

Inigo Vellanoweth would not walk away from tonight's escapade unscathed. Gismond Brenley dismissed his two footmen with strict orders to see to it. The kind Mrs Tetford had been more than happy to oblige him with a report of his daughter's activities in exchange for erasing her husband's rather extensive gaming debt which threatened their ability to stay in London. She'd been prompt, too. It was just after eleven. With luck, his men would find Vellanoweth on his way home.

Brenley poured himself a celebratory drink. It was not a bad night's work, being able to extract retribution from a certain thorn in his side. As to whether or not Audevere had invited Vellanoweth's attentions was not clear. Mrs Tetford could not say, only that Vellanoweth had arrived with Tremblay and Audevere had been all that was proper, right up until Vellanoweth had disappeared into the gardens and Audevere had followed him out.

It did intrigue him to consider what Vellanoweth might want with Audevere. It was no secret to him that Vellanoweth was hunting him, looking for any opportunity for revenge. Last year's debacle had made that clear. Was he looking to seduce information out of Audevere? To turn her head with memories of times past? Or did he seek to ruin her in an attempt to strike out at him? Well, he was about to learn that Audevere had a very protective father.

Chapter Eight

She was holding something back, hiding some key piece of information. It was the only reason Inigo could come up with that explained her reticence on his walk back to Jermyn Street. He'd forgone his carriage in the hope the night air would clear his head. The evening had been enlightening, as had the card party before it. Every time they met, he discovered a new facet of her, was given a new insight into who Audevere Brenley truly was: a young woman who had managed to maintain the hope of a better life even when faced with years of disappointment.

One would never have imagined such depth of character and perseverance lay beneath the surface of the beautiful heiress. One would never have imagined a beautiful heiress would require such qualities. It was easy to believe that beautiful girls had beautiful lives. From what he'd glimpsed, her life had not been beautiful, nor was the term 'disappointments' an adequate word to describe the tragedies she'd suffered: the loss of a beloved mother, leaving behind the quiet life she knew for the glitter of London, entering young womanhood with only an avaricious father to guide her—a father who had not hesitated to use her beauty as a commodity to grease the wheels of his own rise to notoriety and riches.

Inigo kicked at a pebble on the street. It was no wonder her father kept such close watch on her. He wanted to be the sole proprietor of her attentions and Brenley must fear greatly what she could do to him. By running, she was taking away one of his greatest assets. He kicked another pebble, with more force this time, anger heating his blood at thoughts of what she must have endured. She had not shared details, but he hadn't needed them. What she implied was horrific enough.

He had younger sisters, both of a similar age as Audevere when she must have first come to London. He could not fathom his father using them as Audevere had been used. Even if his father had tried, Inigo would not have allowed it. But that was the point. Audevere had had no one to stand up for her. Until now. He would protect her for as long as she would allow it. He was back to the start, where his thoughts had begun: why wouldn't she allow it? He didn't believe it was only thoughts of propriety that held her back, any more than he believed she'd refused his offer of money purely because of her inability to pay him back or her desire not to be beholden to anyone. She wanted no ties. Why? The easy answer was protection. She wanted to protect those around her, but from what? He wasn't afraid of her father, nor did he need protecting from Brenley. What else could there be? Something, that was certain.

What was not certain was how long his willpower would hold out against the onslaught of her temptation. It had lasted this long and it would have to hold a bit longer. Somehow. But his mental fortitude was on its own these days with nothing to hide behind. His carefully constructed barriers had fallen, laid low by Audevere's revelations as early as the Bradfords' ball. In the first days following the loss of Collin, she'd made an obvious and ready target for his grief and his anger. She had killed Collin by breaking off the engagement when she knew he was already hurting. Anger and hate had been convenient emotions to shovel over his own hurt and regret, burying them deep. He'd tried to bury his longing along with the rest. Logic had been his friend. How could he desire a woman who'd killed his best friend? Whom he despised? That barrier had fallen first. She wasn't the enemy. She was as much a victim of Brenley's machinations as Collin or Eliza and as much in need of his help as either of them. Once his mind had understood that, there was no further obstacle to promising his assistance.

As long as Collin had been present, there'd been every reason to restrain himself from pursuing Audevere. But Collin was gone now. No engagement, no best friend, prevented him from taking the kisses

Audevere had offered, or even initiating those kisses himself. All that remained was guilt and honour, and their strength was mightily taxed these days.

He tried to stoke the old guilt as he ticked off the streets towards Jermyn Street, the neighbourhoods quiet, the streets empty in the autumn darkness. No one was about. It seemed as if he had the city to himself as he brought forth the usual arguments: she would always be Collin's former fiancée, that would always remain the foundation of their association. They would not have met if not for Collin. Was it right for him to desire her now that Collin had no claim because he'd also desired her when Collin *had* a legitimate claim? More to the point, was it right to *act* on that desire now that Collin was dead and she was vulnerable? She would have sought comfort in his arms if he'd offered them. The two of them were not foolproof. It had happened before—no comforting had been required as an excuse—just the flimsy façade of a parlour game at a birthday party. He remembered that night as if it were yesterday. It was one of his favourite, and yet most uncomfortable, memories, something to keep him warm as he walked.

It had been late and someone had brandied the punch. Rosenwyn Treleven had been holding court like a queen from her birthday throne. She was eighteen that day and headed to London in a month for her first Season.

'We should play Patipata,' she'd cried. 'Ayleth

shall be Patipata—' she'd named her sister '—and I shall be the blindman calling out the objects and Patipata will say who will kiss them.'

Ayleth had come forward, laughing, and laid her head in Rosenwyn's lap while everyone gathered in a circle.

When all had been ready, Rosenwyn had closed her eyes and pointed unknowingly at her first object—a vase. 'Who shall kiss that, Patipata?'

As Patipata, Ayleth had not been able to see how the circle had organised itself. She'd called a name arbitrarily. 'Cassian!'

Everyone had laughed as Cassian made a grand spectacle of kissing the vase.

On the game had gone, with much humour. Eaton had had to kiss Vennor and Vennor had had to kiss the punch bowl, and Collin had ended up kissing the dog who'd loped in, and so on, until the room had been a riot of laughter, perhaps helped along by the punch in the bowl.

But then, Rosenwyn's unseeing finger had landed on Inigo. 'Patipata, who shall kiss that?'

Inigo had stiffened. He had hoped to escape unnoticed. His friends were so much better at party games than he was, so much more relaxed and willing to do the absurd, to be laughed at and to laugh.

'Audevere shall kiss it,' had come Ayleth's reply.

There had been a general chorus of laughter and oohing, a few comments directed jokingly at Collin. He'd tried to stop it, suggesting that such a thing was inappropriate, that perhaps Collin would mind very much if someone else kissed his intended. But Collin had been no help.

'It's just a game, Inigo, there is no harm in it!' Collin had laughed off the demur.

Audevere had approached, making a bawdy show of it as she crossed the room with an exaggerated swing of her hips and settled down on his lap side-saddle. She'd wet her lips, her eyes locking on his. 'If I didn't know better, I'd think you were afraid to kiss me,' she'd teased.

Not afraid to kiss her—heavens, no. He'd dreamed of kissing her. He'd been afraid he'd like it, that the kiss would live up to the best of his secret fantasies and everyone would know. Worst of all, Collin would know.

She'd leaned in, her mouth capturing his, a soft press of lips against his own. He might have survived that—it had been a simple kiss—but the brandied punch had got the better of the room. Eaton had egged them on, suggesting they could do better than that, and Audevere had always been bold, always up for a lark.

Her arms had gone about his neck, her hands tangling in his hair, and her mouth had opened to him, tempting him. He'd been able to smell her, all vanilla and early spring. He'd felt her, her curves soft against his suddenly not-so-soft body. His blood had run hot and he hadn't been able to resist the chance the game offered. His tongue had sought out hers and she'd answered, hers playing a flirty game of tag with his until the room was hooting and Eaton had called *pax*, Patipata's penance satisfied.

Audevere had slid off his lap and made a playful curtsy to the circle before crossing the room back to Collin's side.

Collin had reached for her and drawn her to him, welcoming her back with a dramatic stage kiss. 'That's my girl. She's up for anything.'

Inigo might as well have been doused with a bucket of cold water. The sight of her in Collin's arms had been reminder enough that their kiss had been all play, while Collin's kiss was real. Very soon, Collin would be her husband and entitled to more than kissing from her.

Only, it hadn't turned out that way. Inigo was here and Collin was gone. The sinner had lived, the saint had died and the damsel between them was in distress. He gave the flames of guilt another hard stoke. Had he wished such a thing into existence? Done something that unconsciously facilitated that reality? Had he ignored a cry for help from Collin? Overlooked some sign? Why did he deserve this chance to claim Audevere? He was the one with the dirty secret, the one who should have been punished. Perhaps he *was* being punished by being forced back into proximity with Audevere, the cause of his sin.

He'd worked hard over the years to try to forget that single kiss. Obviously, he'd been unsuccessful. Did *she* think about it? Or about any of those days?

How she used to tease him for being so serious? How she would lag behind on strolls to try to engage him? To make him laugh? To provoke him? Or was he the only one who kept a visual scrapbook of each moment, each conversation in his mind? Were those encounters easily forgotten by her? A handful of moments in an ocean full of similar moments? Better moments? He should forget them. Perhaps he was ridiculous in holding on to them and ascribing them significance they didn't possess. Although it was hard to believe that based on the last week. Perhaps that was what lay at the heart of the new temptation: he was no longer the only one wanting, desiring. Of course, he could explain the source of her desire. She was in desperate straits and he was her way out. Seeking comfort from him was an entirely natural evolution of her feelings. Eventually, when she was safe, those feelings would fade. But until then, it made things between them deuced difficult.

Inigo's thoughts absorbed him, as desire and logic, past and present, chased each other around in his mind. Too much so. He did not realise he was being followed until it was dangerously late. The three men surrounded him two streets from his rooms, at a place where Jermyn Street crossed with St James's. During the day, the intersection would be bustling, but not this time of night, not in the autumn with fine society out at their hunting boxes in the country. The novelty of having the city to himself was fraught with peril now.

Inigo took the path of least resistance, reaching for his purse, glad he'd given Audevere her share already. He hadn't the patience for cutpurses tonight. He shook it, rattling the coins for them to hear. 'This is what I have, gentlemen.'

'We're not after your money, guv'nor,' the tallest of the three growled, a flick of his hand revealing a sharp-edged knife.

Not the usual cutpurses, then, Inigo thought. The situation immediately turned serious.

'I'm not obliged to offer anything more.' In a fluid motion, Inigo withdrew the blade sheathed in his walking stick.

These were not good odds—three to one in the dark on slippery cobblestones, with no aid in sight—even if he was technically better trained. Cutpurses didn't care if one trained at Jackson's and Manton's. He gave a nod to the tall man with the blade. If he could face each one separately, he had a better chance of dispatching them. Should they decide to rush him all at once, he would be hard-pressed.

'You first, since this was your idea.' Perhaps the tall man was all talk. Perhaps the sight of real steel would help him rethink things.

'Me first, he says, laddies.' The tall man spat into the gutter. 'I'd say we're a bit more democratic than that.'

The trio fanned out and began to advance. Inigo swung hard and suddenly at the man to his right, catching him before he was in position, his blade slicing the man's arm with a deep cut that drew blood and a yelp. The man retreated, clutching his wound.

Inigo pivoted left, his swordstick deflecting the downward slice of the blade just in time before it found his shoulder. He pressed the man back while kicking out at the other assailant, keeping him at a distance, but the other assailant wasn't deterred. He jumped for Inigo, the force of his weight pushing Inigo off balance and taking them both to the ground. It was an ignoble fight now, wrestling and punching on the cobblestones, trying to dodge the man's stabbing blade. His swordstick was too long to be of much use here. Inigo landed a punch to the man's jaw with enough force to push him away so he could scramble to his feet but he'd no sooner gained his legs then the second assailant was on him, grabbing him about the neck from behind.

'Hold him!' The other man was on his feet again, his blade flashing. 'We'll carve him up good.'

Inigo fought, twisting and turning to dislodge his captor, but the man had the strength of a vice. One thought passed through his mind as he struggled: he was going to die in a fashionable alley, stabbed to death like his mentor Richard Penlerick had been over a year ago. No, not tonight. Not when Audevere needed him, not when he hadn't got revenge for Collin. There was too much to do to die tonight.

He brought his foot down hard on his captor's instep, making him squeal in pain and loosen his grip, enough for him to break free and to plough, head down like a bull, into the stomach of the on-coming attacker, his momentum causing the man's blade to come free of his hand and skitter away on the cobblestones.

There was a yell behind him, followed by the sounds of combat, fists on flesh, as Inigo finished off his own opponent with a blow to the jaw. The man slumped to the ground. Inigo turned to manage the last thug only to find him already dispatched by his unlooked-for ally. The man was dressed all in black and wore a mask over his face. 'You! You're the Vigilante,' Inigo panted in disbelief. He leaned against a wall, catching his breath and studying the man before him. For the past year, a man had been reported roaming the streets, meting out his own rough justice. 'So you're not just a rumour, a fanciful figment of bored society's imagination.' Inigo grinned his gratitude. 'I am glad for it. I am indebted to you.' He held out his hand, but the man did not take it. The man did not speak. He simply nodded and disappeared into the night.

Inigo brushed off his clothes and gave himself a quick assessment. Other than the rips sustained by his clothing and a collection of scrapes, he was far less injured than he might have been if the Vigilante hadn't shown up when he did. But that reassurance did little to calm his nerves or settle his mind. His body pulsed with the restless energy that follows combat and his mind was a riot of emotions and questions, not the least of which was utter disbelief:

he was a peer of the realm, Earl of Tintagel, heir to a dukedom. Only the boldest of the bold would think to assault him. Assuming, of course, that the bold knew who he was. But they must have known! They'd not been interested in his heavy purse. What sort of cutpurse chose to beat a man instead of taking the volunteered money and fleeing?

These were not cutpurses; these were thugs and they'd been sent specifically to target him.

The conclusion flashed through his hot mind like Vauxhall fireworks, followed by another flare: Brenley. Who else would be bold enough? Who else would *want* to do such a thing to him? He was not in the habit of making enemies. There were only so many reasons Brenley would have done it. Somehow, Brenley had known Audevere had been meeting him or perhaps he didn't like the threat to the proposal he hoped Tremblay would soon be making and he thought to send a warning.

Inigo steadied himself with a hand against the wall of a building. Was Brenley warning him, or was Brenley warning her? Which meant he suspected she was planning something. A tremor passed through him that had nothing to do with his recent brush with danger. This tremor was all for Audevere. If she was truly in peril, three days might be too long to wait. Her escape might be cut off before it even had a chance.

He could not go back to his rooms. Spending a night alone with his thoughts would accomplish nothing. He turned his feet towards Newlyn House. He needed Vennor and he needed a cooler head than his at the moment to think things through. Never mind it was past midnight. That was what friends were for.

Chapter Nine

'Inigo, what has happened?' One look at him was enough to send Vennor into action. One could always count on Vennor to do *something*. He wasn't one for sitting around idly. Within moments, footmen were called, the kitchen was awakened, tea was brewed, decanters refreshed. 'Do you need a physician?' Vennor pressed a generously filled tumbler into his hands, looking rather pale himself. He must look worse than he thought if Vennor resembled a ghost. He peered at Vennor as his friend moved about the room giving orders. No, not a ghost. Vennor's brow was sweaty, his hair tousled from the outdoors, not from sleep, Inigo would wager. Had he caught his friend coming in from an evening out? But his mind had little time for Vennor's dishevelled, frantic appearance.

'It happened at St James's and Jermyn. I was nearly home.' Inigo sipped his drink gratefully. The post-combat thrill was leaving him and he was feeling the effects of the drubbing he'd taken. 'There were three of them and I hadn't been paying attention. They took me quite unaware.' That had been *his* mistake. He'd set himself up to be an ideal mark. 'But here's where it gets interesting. They didn't want my money. I offered my purse straight away, but they made it plain they had come for *me*.'

'You could have been killed.' Vennor settled on the edge of his chair.

'The thought did cross my mind, at the time,' Inigo replied drily. 'The one thought I had as I stood there with my swordstick was that I might die just like your father—stabbed at a fashionable crossroads by street thugs.' He shuddered.

'Thank God you weren't. I've lost too many people I've loved.' Vennor had paled considerably at the mention. Perhaps he should not have mentioned Vennor's parents? Or was it more than that? Vennor's eyes had a shuttered quality to them, hiding whatever was going on in his mind.

'God might have had something to do with it, but more directly, I owe emerging largely unscathed to the Vigilante. He showed up. Just in time, too. Otherwise things might have ended differently. I was getting the pulp beaten out of me and I was outnumbered.' It was easier to talk about the assault if he could imbue the details with a certain insouciance.

'The Vigilante showed up?' Vennor replied. 'I'm glad for it. My father wouldn't have wanted you to meet your end as he did.'

'How is that going?' Inigo asked cautiously. By 'that' he meant Vennor's investigation into his parents' untimely deaths. It was an awkward and touchy subject. He didn't quite know how to talk to Vennor about it. 'Do you have any new leads on who might have done it?'

It. That. Neutral, nondescript terms. Richard's memory deserved better than hesitant rhetoric from him.

'No, nothing.' Vennor shook his head with a sigh. 'The trail is likely frigid by now.' Frigid was too intense a term and it alerted Inigo immediately to the lie. Vennor was hiding something. He'd spent a year and a half looking for the killers. He would not suddenly capitulate and give up. But Vennor was in no mood to talk about his own investigation.

'We're getting off topic,' Vennor redirected. 'I think it's safe to conclude Gismond Brenley was behind tonight's attack.'

'Yes, I'd already thought of that. It's Audevere I'm worried about now.' He slipped off his coat and shirt, taking the clean clothes offered by a footman. Inigo imbued his words with a certain nonchalance. He had things he wanted to hide, too. He didn't want Vennor to think his emotions were engaged or that there were feelings for Audevere that might cloud his thinking. He was aware enough of what risks those factors might pose.

Vennor slanted him an *I-told-so-you* eyebrow. 'No, it's not like that.' Inigo leapt to Audevere's defence.

'I am concerned she's in danger, that this attack was meant to send a message. I need to get her out of that house and get her away while there's still time.'

Vennor pushed his blond hair back from his face and let out a low breath. 'She's got you wrapped around her finger, doesn't she? You're just going to whisk her away? Her father will come after you.'

'Probably. But it's time this underground feud between Brenley and the Dukes ended and it's high time that Brenley's behaviour is exposed. We have nothing to fear from him. We can come forward.' Inigo laid out his plan. 'I want to leave the letter for the King with you. You can deliver it if my threat isn't taken seriously.' Or if something happened to him because the threat was taken all too seriously.

'You trust her, then? And she's worth this risk?' Vennor asked cautiously. Inigo could sense the search for understanding in his tone.

'She is,' Inigo answered evenly, holding his friend's gaze. A few weeks ago he would have answered differently. He would have said Audevere was ancillary to the project of avenging Collin or exposing Brenley. That taking her away was just another method of striking back at him. But that had changed in the wake of Audevere's story. This was becoming more about seeing her safe than it was about avenging Collin's death.

'Are you falling in love with her?' Vennor couldn't keep the worry from his voice. Inigo understood how this looked to his friend. The daughter of their enemy was once more setting her sights on one of their number. The recipe for disaster was obvious.

So much for hiding his emotional attachment. 'I care for her, Vennor,' Inigo confessed. 'She has been through hell and if we do not get her away, she will continue to suffer. I know how this sounds to you; I know you doubt her. But don't doubt me. My word has always been enough for you and I'm counting on my word being enough for you now when I tell you we hardly knew her. She is so much more, has endured so much more, than we ever could have guessed.'

Vennor was silent for a long while. Then, slowly, he nodded his head. 'You're right. I don't know her. I *can* only take your word for it that she needs you. More than that, I can only take your word that she is not leading you into trouble. I do not want to see you hurt, my friend. But your word is all I need. What can I do?'

Inigo grinned, feeling better than he had all night. 'Thank you, Ven. I owe you.'

'No, you don't. Friends don't owe.' Ven shook his head. 'You were all there for me when my parents died. I wouldn't have got through that first week without each of you. I can never repay that debt.'

'Very well.' Inigo nodded his acceptance and began to plan. 'We'll need to get Tremblay involved. Brenley will never believe a summons if it comes from us…' His plan would go into motion in just eight hours. He hoped it would be soon enough to spare Audevere.

* * *

Gismond Brenley eyed his daughter over the edge of his newspapers at breakfast. He would know soon enough if Audevere was guilty of deliberately attracting Inigo Vellanoweth's attentions last night. He hoped not. It would mean his hold on her was slipping, that she no longer feared what he could expose about her. The sooner he could marry her off to Viscount Tremblay the better and then his grip on her would be strong once again.

He rattled his newspapers to get her attention. 'Mrs Tetford said Tremblay was happy to see you last night,' he mentioned benignly.

'Yes, the company last night was very pleasant.' Audevere looked up briefly from her breakfast with a polite half-smile, her expression bland. If she was hiding anything, she was doing it well.

'Inigo Vellanoweth was with him, I hear. I also hear he ran into a bit of trouble on the way home. He was set upon by thugs.' Never mind those thugs had been less effective than Brenley had hoped. Vellanoweth had put up quite the resistance and then the damned Vigilante had interrupted. Still, he was assured a few punches had been landed before help had arrived; enough damage had been done to ensure that his message had been received.

'He was beaten?' Audevere's voice held a tinge of unmistakable worry. Perhaps it was only from natural concern, but perhaps not.

'Oh, yes,' he assured her nonchalantly from behind his papers as if it was of no consequence to him. 'First Richard Penlerick is killed in the streets and now this attack on Vellanoweth. One might think those Cornish Dukes are unlucky.'

One might think such a thing indeed if one didn't know better. Audevere tried to keep her expression and responses normal. She forced herself to keep buttering her toast. Inigo had been attacked. Even now, Inigo was hurting. He would know who'd sent the men. Would he blame her? Would he think she'd betrayed him? Was he cursing the day he'd agreed to help her? She wanted to run from the room, right into the street, and keep running until she reached him. She wanted to assure herself he was all right. But she could give away not even the slightest indication of her feelings without betraying him in truth.

This was her fault. She'd not been as safe as she'd thought at the musicale. Someone had seen them sneak out. Someone had reported them. Inigo's beating was a message to her. Her father suspected something, but what and how much? Three days seemed like an eternity now. She felt sick to her stomach. Inigo had been hurt because of her! But perhaps now he'd believe her when she warned him, when she expressed reticence about dragging him into her life. Perhaps now he'd be glad she'd refused the cottage in Devonshire.

A footman entered the room and offered her father the salver with a message on it. She watched his face move from confusion to satisfaction as he broke the seal and scanned it. 'We have good news, Daughter. Viscount Tremblay has an investment opportunity he wants to share with me.' He tapped the edge of the note on the table. 'He wants me to meet with his investors in Dover. He's invited me to travel with him. The only catch is that he's leaving tomorrow. That doesn't give me much time and I hate to leave you. But I think there's no choice. He says he means to go on to his home in Sussex afterward.'

She could see her father weighing the opportunity with the risk. Not to see Tremblay one more time would be to forfeit his suit. Once in Sussex, Tremblay would be tucked in for the winter. London would not see the Viscount again until spring and Cornwall was even further from Sussex than it was from London. They would lose him, possibly permanently. Everyone knew Tremblay's neighbour had a pretty daughter and a large adjoining estate. Audevere remained silent. If she was too eager to have her father pursue the trip with the Viscount, she would rouse his suspicions. And she had a few of those herself. The offer couldn't have come at a more opportune time. Just when she needed her father out of the house, here he was with a coveted invitation to leave for Dover. Now her hand really did still on the butter knife. The game was afoot.

The footman returned, this time with a bouquet of flowers. 'For you, miss. Courtesy of the Viscount.'

Her father brightened considerably at the prospect. 'It looks like the Viscount is back.' Audevere tried to see the morning's deliveries through her father's eyes: the gesture of flowers was a sign of continued courtship and matrimonial interest; the invitation for a shared investment a sign that Inigo's earlier visit to the Viscount had not deterred him from pursuit; the request to travel together a chance to continue more private conversations before the Viscount decamped for the winter.

She smiled coyly. 'Perhaps he never left, Father. I told you that waltz at the Bradfords' would spark him to action. There's nothing like a little competition to remind a man of what he wants. It's what you told me to do and I did it.' She rose, flowers in hand. 'Might I be excused to find a vase for them?'

He waved her away, hardly noticing, his mind already arranging his trip to Dover with the Viscount. There was no question of not going now. How he must be revelling, Audevere thought as she left the room in search of a vase and some privacy. Her father had spent a lifetime hoping for such opportunities.

Audevere found a private alcove in which to read the card that came with the bouquet. At first it was a disappointment. It actually was from Tremblay—but surely Inigo would have spoken to him by now, as he had promised? It read simply and predictably.

I look forward to your father's company in Dover and to seeing you again. Please respond

*with an appropriate time to call upon you for
a private meeting.*

It was signed *Arthur Fenmore, Fourth Viscount
Tremblay.* Only the four was written in Roman nu-
merals: IV.

There was no need to indicate he was the fourth
of that title in such an unusual fashion. Except...
IV didn't only stand for four. It also stood for Inigo
Vellanoweth.

Audevere smiled in relief. She'd not imagined it.
Tremblay would be the go-between and the decoy.
Tremblay would take her father to Dover and make
sure he stayed there. And Tremblay would deliver
her response to Inigo. But she'd have to write today,
before Tremblay left. She folded the note carefully
and breathed a sigh of relief. Inigo was all right and
he had a plan. Inigo had not forsaken her even after
last night's beating.

She berated herself for the doubt, remembering Inigo's confidence last night, how intoxicating he'd been in that moment. Here it was, only the
next morning, and he'd put a plan into action, perhaps worried for her after last night's events despite
what had happened to him. The thought made her
throat thick. How long had it been since anyone had
had a care for her? Had there been anyone since her
mother died, since Collin died? Everyone who cared
for her had a habit of dying. Her father had sent men
to attack Inigo. To scare her, to scare him. It hadn't

worked. It had only served to further entrench her determination, and Inigo's, too, it seemed, to get her away. Audevere touched the note in her pocket with a sense of relief. She wasn't alone any more.

Chapter Ten

It galled Inigo that he couldn't get to her. He'd managed to send her father away and he still couldn't claim her. He slammed down the articulating compartments of his telescope as Tremblay's carriage drew away from the kerb in front of Brenley House. Tremblay and Brenley were off to Dover, Tremblay more than willing to play the decoy for a few days in exchange for Inigo having warned him off the match. Tremblay's sister went with them, adding to the authenticity. But that didn't mean the way was clear for Inigo to storm the castle or for Audevere to leave it.

He handed the telescope to Vennor. Audevere had been right. She was watched at every turn by servants and Inigo knew who owned the servants' loyalty. The house was a veritable fortress. Brenley could leave in full confidence that his daughter would go nowhere undetected, receive no one unchaperoned. Not that one would notice how carefully she was watched. It was all discreetly done. He waited for Vennor to survey the landscape from their position across the street, wanting a second opinion.

'There are four men who walk the street,' Vennor confirmed. Which meant that someone was passing in front of the house every five minutes and that the house was always in view both front and back to someone. He handed the telescope back to Inigo and grimaced. 'Anyone trying to get in will be noticed approaching the house, even from the back. We can't storm the castle, not without giving ourselves away, and the odds would be against us, two on four assuming no one else joins in.'

Calling attention to the escape was the last thing Inigo wanted. The more time between Audevere's disappearance and its discovery and sending word to Gismond Brenley the better. With luck, they might already be in Cornwall before Brenley returned to London. And then the letter would be waiting for him, a shield against him racing to Cornwall to drag his daughter back. 'If we can't go in, she'll have to come out.' He opened his pocket watch and studied the watch face. 'The delivery will be here in half an hour.' The delivery was a bouquet of flowers, nominally from Tremblay, with a small envelope of powder tucked inside meant for the guards. Inigo didn't like putting it all in Audevere's hands, or risking someone opening the note and becoming suspicious. Not because she was helpless—she was far from that. He just preferred having more control. He wanted to be there if anything went wrong.

Now, all he could do was wait. The hours until to-night would seem endless.

Vennor clapped him on the shoulder. 'Let's go to Manton's and shoot something. Time will pass more quickly if we stay busy and it wouldn't hurt if word got out that you were practising.' No, it wouldn't, Inigo acknowledged. There was a hypothesis among London's gentlemen that shooting well at Manton's in front of a crowd was often the best deterrent to being called out for a duel.

'If Brenley saw you shoot today, he'd think twice before issuing a challenge.' Vennor chuckled as Inigo took up his position, arm extended, body in profile, and sighted the wafer at the end of the lane. He fired with exacting precision, the paper wafer on the target showing a hole. A smattering of applause broke out along the perimeter of the shooting gallery. Twenty-Seven Davies Street, home to Manton's, was busy for an afternoon out of season. Inigo and Vennor had shared a lane, putting on an impromptu shooting clinic as they practised slow shots with smooth-bore barrelled pistols.

'That makes eighteen culped for me out of twenty, to your fifteen,' Inigo said, stepping back so Vennor could take his last shot.

'Soon to be sixteen,' Vennor corrected confidently as a boy ran to replace the wafer. 'I'll make this shot, not that it matters. There was no beating you today.' Normally, they split their expertise between them—

Vennor with guns and Inigo with rapiers. But today, Inigo had been intent on excellence. If Brenley chose to duel, he wouldn't pick rapiers. Inigo would need the ability to summon one good shot.

Vennor took his shot, hitting the wafer. 'Told you I'd hit it.' He grinned as they handed their pistols off to a waiting page. They put on their jackets and headed out in search of a drink. Outside, a sharp breeze made the late afternoon cold. 'Do you think it will come to pistols?' Vennor asked once they were alone and could talk seriously.

'I would almost prefer that, but there's no guarantee Brenley will play fair.' He'd rather not live with the fear of looking over his shoulder, of waiting for another assault to come. Getting Audevere away tonight had to be secretive, but there would be no hiding it or his involvement for long, not once the letter was read. What had begun as one woman's attempt to sneak away from home unobserved had become open warfare. Tonight, he and Audevere would start the four-day journey to Cornwall and the battle would be fully engaged. Inigo drew the collar of his greatcoat up to ward off the chill, a reminder that fall was fully upon them.

Inigo jerked his head towards the inn, hoping for a distraction. There were still hours until tonight, five of them to be precise, before he could effect his rescue of Audevere. 'Shall we call in at the Running Horse for an early dinner?' It would be his last dinner with Vennor for a while.

* * *

Once settled inside, Vennor stared at him, hard. 'I don't know the last time I've seen you in love—or if I ever have. Although I thought there was someone once, years ago. But you never said anything and nothing ever came of it.' Vennor paused, understanding he was on intimate ground. 'What becomes of this after?' To his credit, Vennor asked carefully, 'Is this an affair or something more permanent?'

Inigo shook his head. 'I don't know. She insists on cutting all ties once she reaches safety.' He understood that she was afraid, but he had faith in the strength of the protection he and his family and friends could offer her.

Vennor gave a wry smile. 'But you think otherwise. I see it in your face.' He reached across the table and squeezed Inigo's forearm in brotherly commiseration. 'I hope it works out for you. Shall we go and fetch her?'

'We?' Inigo looked surprised as he laid down coins for their meal. He'd thought Vennor would say goodbye here.

'You didn't think I'd let you face Brenley House alone, did you? We'll pick up my horse and I'll travel with you as far as the outskirts of London.' There would be just enough time to make a detour to the Newlyn Mews to get Vennor's horse. The time that had dragged all day was suddenly starting to fly. Inigo checked off items in his mind: ready Vennor's horse, meet the travelling coach, which he'd packed

this morning, then be in position to pull up outside
Brenley House at quarter past nine. He was glad of
Vennor's presence. Vennor was good in a fight, as
he'd proven throughout their childhood. What they
found at the Brenley town house would depend on
how successful Audevere had been. But successful
or not, they weren't leaving there without her. It was
tonight or not at all.

Audevere slipped the powder into the mulled wine
and stirred the mugs quickly. She had only so much
privacy between the kitchen where Cook had mixed
the evening draughts for her father's men and the
mews at the back which they all eventually passed
on their circuit around Brenley House. It had been
difficult enough to convince Cook she wanted to deliver the tray personally to thank them for their efforts to protect her in the absence of her father. She
took a deep breath to steady her nerves and checked
the time again. Eight o'clock. By the time all the men
had been served it would be half past. That would
give the powder three-quarters of an hour to work
for and the house to settle for the night. The last was
up to her. If she retired early, it would give a cue to
the staff that they could retire as well.

Audevere stepped out into the night with her
tray. The sooner the men were served, the sooner
she could begin. The sooner she could walk out her
front door. And Inigo would be waiting.

That one thought got her through delivering the

wine. It got her upstairs; it got her through waiting for the house to quiet. Even Patsy, who could likely be trusted, had been sent to bed. That had been the hardest of all: saying goodnight to Patsy as she had every night for eight years and pretending she'd see her in the morning. But she didn't want Patsy to be implicated in anything when her father found out she was gone.

Now she was alone in her room, a single valise packed for her new life. She didn't dare try to take more. She needed to move quickly, silently when the time came. And if she met anyone on her way down the stairs, she needed to be ready to leave the valise behind if she had to run for it. Dear lord, she hoped that wouldn't happen. Her palms were sweaty as the last minutes ticked by. She rubbed them on her skirts, looked at her room one last time, picked up her valise and made her way into the hall.

The walk along the landing to the stairs, down the stairs, and across the hall to the door, had never seemed so long. Her ears were alert to any creak of the floor, every sound of her footsteps. She made it to the door, shutting it carefully and quietly behind her, her heart hammering. She took in the street, sweeping it for any sign of the men, any sign the powder had not worked. But it was the sight of Inigo's dark coach across the street that brought her the most relief. The lanterns were not lit, but she could make him out beside it, dressed in his greatcoat. She began to run, her body shivering as she crossed the street—

from the cold, from nerves, from the enormity of what she'd chosen to do. But somehow she knew that if she could just reach him, all would be well.

Inigo reached out to take the valise from her, hefting it in one hand. 'Is this all?' He stowed it beneath a seat and helped her in, as eager as she to be underway without being noticed.

'All I could carry.' She gave a smile as if the joke came easily to her. In truth, it had been difficult to choose which few items to take with her—which dresses, which shoes, which accessories would serve her best in her new life. She settled in her seat, Inigo giving the signal to go to Vennor, who rode up next to the coachman.

'You were expecting trouble. You brought Vennor.' She tried to hide her trembling hands in the folds of her skirt, but nothing escaped Inigo's notice.

'You're shaking, Aud.' He drew out a travelling rug and tucked it about her lap, taking her hands in his. 'You'll be warm soon. That will help.' His gaze held hers with reassurance. 'Don't be frightened, Aud.'

'I'm not shaking because I'm frightened.' There was even a tremor in her voice and her mouth was dry. 'I'm shaking because I'm free. For the first time since my mother died, I'm free.' Free. And alone, at the mercy of her wits with nothing more than four dresses, a hairbrush and a bag of odds and ends to her name. It was an overwhelming mixture of excitement and fear. So much was uncertain. There would be danger down this path she'd chosen, and risk. But there would also be the opportunity of happiness, of reclaiming a kind of purity that had eluded her until now.

'Free doesn't mean you have to be alone.' Inigo divined her thoughts so easily these days. 'I *will* take care of you.'

Of course he would. That was what Inigo did. He'd taken care of Collin, he'd taken care of Eliza Blaxland, and now he would take care of her. If she'd let him. She had to be careful what she allowed or she would find it too hard to leave when the time came. But for now, the thought of being taken care of was too wonderful to fight against and it made her throat tighten and her eyes sting with tears of gratitude. A little gasp escaped her as the magnitude of what she'd done overwhelmed her and her tears began to spill, impossible to be contained any longer. She pressed a hand to her mouth in embarrassment and in a moment of panic. 'What I have done?' she whispered as Inigo gathered her into his arms.

'The only thing you could, my dear,' he murmured. It occurred to her, as the coach pulled away into the night, that if she could have only one person with her in this mad bid for freedom, she would want it to be Inigo. As long as he was beside her, surely anything was possible. Perhaps something of him was wearing off on her, after all.

Chapter Eleven

The scent of her assailed him in soft waves where she had fallen asleep against his shoulder somewhere around midnight, slowly permeating the carriage throughout the night. It was a kind of sensual torture to have her so near: the smell of her in his nostrils; the weight of her head on his shoulder despite its own stiff discomfort from the beating; the knowledge that she was relying on him and yet that reliance that had brought her to him would lead to a permanent parting if she had her way.

She shifted against him in sleep and he adjusted his position to accommodate her. He had four days to change her mind, to show her that there was another way. And that way was with him. *With him.* The words carried a sense of finality with them. He would keep her safe, not just for a week or a few months, but for all time, in ways that he'd failed to keep Collin safe.

What did that safety look like? The cottage in

Devonshire or something more? His conscience would only allow for the cottage, but his heart wanted something more.

Marry her. Reach out and seize all you've ever wanted. You've waited for this for years and now it's within your grasp.

But could he ever be happy with the woman he'd secretly coveted when she'd belonged to his best friend?

He stroked back a piece of hair from her face, watching her sleep. She was at peace for the moment. It had been easy to justify helping her escape. Collin would want him to help her and it was the honourable thing to do. But now those motives forked. How could he marry her and not feel guilty about it for the rest of his life? Such guilt would blight their happiness, poison them. Perhaps it would be best to let her go, to convince them both the cottage in Devonshire was the best either of them could hope for.

She stirred again, waking as dawn approached, embarrassed at having fallen asleep against him. 'Have you been awake the entire time? You should have woken me, or at least moved me so you could have slept.'

'I have all day to nap if needed and I wanted to keep watch.' In case the men at the town house awoke, in case they discovered her missing before this morning. But there'd been no chase. They were safe for now.

Audevere pulled aside a curtain and looked out at

the bleak landscape, nothing more than grey shadows in the slowly lightening landscape. 'The first sunrise of my new life.' She smiled at him with satisfaction. 'It feels good. I am never going back, Inigo. I will never be his again.'

Of course not. He wouldn't allow it. This was one thing on which they could both agree and for now it was enough.

They stopped at a small posting inn to break their fast and water the horses at around eight. The day was proving to be cold and grey, the miles stretching out endlessly before them. 'We'll stop at a proper inn tonight and have a decent meal and comfortable beds,' Inigo assured her as they set off again.

'But until then, how shall we pass the time?' Audevere asked, a coy look in her eye that suggested she had an idea. She reached into the pocket of her travelling skirt and pulled out a deck of cards. 'Shall we play? I am passably good at piquet.'

Inigo laughed. 'You might be the only person I know who would run away with a deck of cards. Luckily for you, I am also passably good at piquet.' He'd seen her play whist at the Thurstons'. He'd bet his purse she was more than passable at any card game.

He'd have made a good return on that wager, Inigo thought a few hours later. As it turned out, they were both more than adequate at the game and were both more than exceedingly competitive. They played away the morning and past lunch. They might have played on into the afternoon if the horses hadn't needed to be rested and the driver spelled. They chose a spot by a river and got out to stretch their legs. The clouds overhead had not cleared, but hung low and heavy in the sky, promising rain. Inigo grimaced. The rain would slow them down.

'You play well. How did you learn?' Inigo complimented her as they walked alongside the river.

'My mother taught me when I was very young. We didn't have many entertainments beyond our own company, so we spent a lot of time together, playing.' There was fondness in her voice, as there had been the night she'd handed him the jewels. Whoever Lady Brenley had been, she'd held her daughter's heart.

Back inside the carriage, Inigo laid out a modest picnic of sorts. 'There's bread and meat and cheese. I had everything sliced ahead of time. I didn't trust myself to do the job in a moving carriage, not with roads like these.'

'You really do think of everything, don't you? I think that's the key to your thoughtfulness, all this attention to detail.' Audevere flashed him a grateful smile that warmed him more thoroughly than any lap robe or brick could do.

'And gratefulness is the key to yours.' Inigo returned the smile. 'You needn't thank me for everything. I am happy to do it, happy to provide whatever you need, Aud.' He held her gaze, steady

in the bouncing vehicle. 'It is a privilege to help you.'
The carriage confines seemed to grow closer, the air
igniting with the flame that managed too often to
crackle to life between them. He wanted to touch her,
wanted to kiss her, wanted to tell her that she need
not worry about anything ever again. But those were
the promises of a schoolboy. They were not promises
he could keep when so much was uncertain. Meanwhile, want and desire were likely to kill him. How
far they'd come from sparring on the Bradfords' veranda, vying for one another's trust. Now that they
had it, what would they do with it?

Perhaps Audevere felt the tension, too. 'I *am*
grateful to you, Inigo.' She laughed, a breathy little
sound. 'Besides, my mother raised me to be polite,
to say please and thank you.' There was a little coy
sassiness behind the remark and it did the trick,
pushing the tension to the back burner once more.

Inigo helped himself to another slice of bread and
cheese. 'You've spoken well of your mother on two
occasions now. Tell me about her, this paragon of
motherhood who taught her daughter manners and
card playing.' He smiled and stretched out his legs,
crossing them at the ankles, trying not to look avaricious. But he was greedy for any piece of Audevere he could get. He wanted to know her, wanted
her stories, all of them. Even the bad ones. Perhaps
in those stories he'd find the clue to her resistance,
the reason why she wouldn't consider living under
his protection in the Devonshire cottage.

* * *

He wanted something from her, more than a story of her mother. It was a thought that left her both warm and wary at the prospect.

Go carefully with this one, her mind whispered. *Men always want something. That's how men work.*

Even Inigo? It was a question today, not a statement as it might have been a few weeks ago, a testament to how much things had changed between them, how her own feelings had changed regarding him. He was something far more personal to her now than just someone who might help her. She'd not gone to him looking for this level of attachment, yet there was no denying it was there or that it was growing. It wasn't merely attachment any more, it was affection, trust. She felt safe with him, as she'd felt with no other man.

'Tell me a story, Aud,' Inigo cajoled. 'We've hours to go before evening.' The slow drawl of the request coupled with the full attention of his Boscastle blue eyes was irresistible.

'It might not be as exciting as you think,' she teased. But she'd already decided. She would tell him of her childhood in Truro. She would bring her mother to life for him. Surely she could do that without exposing too much of herself, secrets and all.

Audevere drew a deep breath, sorting through her thoughts. Where to start? Not at the very beginning. That was the secret she wanted to hide the most. 'As you know, my father was a sea captain before he was knighted. He wasn't in the Navy. He was a private captain, merchant and cargo ships mostly. He was gone most of my childhood. It was just me and my mother at our home outside Truro,' She stopped. 'You know this already. See, I told you the story would be boring.'

'Hardly,' Inigo assured her. 'Besides, I'm a patient man. And I'm reasonably assured it will get more interesting.' He offered her a wry smile that made her swat at his boots in a playful scold before she continued.

'My father would visit when he was home. He'd sail up the estuary to the cottage and bring us presents, but we always held our breath until he left again. Thankfully, he was restless. He never stayed long. Just long enough to leave a little money and make sure we were well and quiet. He wanted us to live quietly. He was very explicit about that.' She hadn't understood the reasons for that until years later. 'Living quietly suited us. We walked to Truro for church on Sunday and whenever we needed to visit the market, but other than that we kept to ourselves.' She smiled at the look on Inigo's face. 'I see I've surprised you. You cannot imagine me as a hermit...' she paused '...or that I had a decent childhood? I did.' Very decent. Even now, she could conjure in her mind the little limestone cottage with its thatched roof, the small garden set to the side where her mother grew carrots and beans and a row of corn.

What riches they'd had in the summers when their little crops were ready to eat.

'Life was very different before 1814, Inigo. I had a mother. She taught me herself how to read, how to write, how to think. We took long walks, picked wildflowers, we bird-watched in the estuary. She taught me all the names of the plants and herbs and what they were good for. I was content. My father was a temperamental man, never happy, always wanting more, always plotting to get more, but I gave him no heed. He was a black cloud that seldom sailed through my life and was quickly gone.'

'I never knew Lady Brenley,' Inigo prompted gently. 'She sounds like a good mother.'

She was, more than Inigo could ever know, but Audevere would not share that part of the story. 'I miss her every day,' Audevere said softly. There were countless nights she wished for her mother's counsel, her strength. She fell silent. Outside, the raindrops pattered against the windows. 'I've often wondered what she saw in my father, to marry him. They were such opposites,' she offered idly. 'Perhaps she saw what many women see in a husband: security, shelter, someone to care for their needs.' She looked at Inigo. 'I don't think he loved her. And I don't think she loved him.'

'They had you; there must have been some affection at some time,' Inigo offered.

After a fashion…they'd had her. But she'd not planned on telling that part of the story. Instead,

Audevere said, 'She died right after my father received his knighthood for his heroic services in the Peninsular War. My father made his money in the wars, you know, running arms, supplying the troops, smuggling. I didn't understand all that until much later. All I knew was that after the war, we had money, a title and a town house in London. 'My mother never saw it.' She gave a little laugh to lighten the mood, her happy story having become maudlin. 'Perhaps that was best. My father has expensive but gaudy taste.'

But Inigo wouldn't let her stray from the story line. His tone was soft beneath the raindrop patter. 'How did she die?' Did Inigo realise she never discussed this with anyone? Or that no one ever asked? Her mother had simply been erased. It was a kind of blessing that someone wanted to know now and a double blessing that the person who wanted to know was Inigo, a man who knew deep loss of his own, who would know without the necessity of words what that loss had meant to her.

Her own voice was as quiet as the road and rain allowed. 'Suddenly. A fever, an illness that took her in two nights. She'd been fine one day and ill the next. We'd played cards the night before.' Audevere swallowed against a surge of emotion before adding, 'For the last time. She let me win.'

'I was right,' Inigo said quietly. 'She was wonderful. Far more wonderful than I. I would never just let you win.' He grinned and his soft humour was exactly what she required to get over the thickness in her throat, this man who always seemed to know what she needed. He gave her a moment before asking, 'Then you came up to London?' This was more than she'd planned on telling. This was a different story.

'Yes. Conveniently, with our new wealth, my father didn't have to go to sea any longer to make his living and I needed a guardian.' The sweetness of her life had vanished overnight. 'I was fourteen and becoming a beauty, in my father's opinion—and in the opinion of his friends as well.' She watched Inigo's body go on alert. She'd alluded to some of this earlier.

This part was harder to tell: how she'd gone from reclusive country girl to budding London beauty, how her father had not hesitated to exploit that, how he would have her sit at his table to act as his hostess when he held business suppers. If anyone questioned the propriety of such an arrangement, he excused it with a wave of his hand and an easy laugh, saying a sea captain didn't know any better; besides, he had no wife to play the hostess and wasn't his daughter pretty decked out in her frocks?

He'd loved dressing her as if she were already a woman: gowns no girl not yet out would wear, hair piled up as if for a night at the opera, pearl earrings in her ears, sometimes even diamond studs. Audevere's chin went up in a flash of defensiveness. 'And I liked it.' There was the guilt, the shame, the familiar

self-loathing. She gave Inigo a tremulous, apologetic
smile. She had only herself to blame. She'd allowed
so much, not knowing any better.

'Of course you did,' Inigo offered something akin
to absolution in his words and it warmed her. 'What
young girl doesn't like dressing up? My sisters beg
to wear fine gowns and jewels. My mother has the
devil's own time curbing their tendencies towards
grandeur.' He had sisters. What a lovely thought, one
she would tuck away for later when she was alone
and missing him. She would imagine him with his
family, his sisters, laughing together, loving each
other. A normal family.

'Perhaps I liked it too much, though.' She hesitated to accept his absolution. 'I was glad to make
my father happy. He blustered less, yelled less, complained less. I was pleased to play at being hostess
and imagining myself the grand lady. I didn't see any
reason to protest. I was naive and I was having fun.'
She looked down at her hands. 'His friends liked me,
too. They saw nothing wrong with a fifteen-year-
old dressed beyond her years acting as a hostess.
They encouraged it. They brought me presents—rib-
bons, hairpins, small pieces of jewellery or a box of
bon-bons—and *I* encouraged that. I loved the gifts
and the attention. Growing up alone, never having
any friends, I was intoxicated by this new life full
of luxuries where I was the centre of so much attention. I didn't see the danger in it. The men were so
kind, so interested in me, and their interest pleased

my father, a man who'd been a stranger to me all my life and who was the only family I had left.'

She stopped there and held Inigo's gaze. She wanted to warn him. The story turned dark here. 'But I learned quickly that no man gives anything without expecting something in return.' She watched the realisation take him. Inigo's eyes froze, his body tensed as if to do battle.

'You don't mean to say they...' He groped for a word. Even as frank as he usually was, he couldn't bring himself to say it. He was looking for a polite word, but there were no polite words for what she implied.

'That they importuned me? Oh, yes. But it was my fault. I encouraged them through my efforts to engage their attention.' Even now, she wondered if there'd been something she should have done differently. If there'd been something she should have known? If it would have happened that way if her mother had lived? If she'd had her mother's guidance? But she'd had no one to tell her how to go on. 'At first, they felt entitled to stolen kisses, but later they felt entitled to more.' Over-friendly touches, indiscreetly long glimpses down the front of her dress, that had escalated to fondling—even a few requests that she be the one doing the touching and fondling. Sometimes in an alcove while conversations carried on beyond the thin curtain.

'Surely your father wouldn't allow such behaviour,' Inigo broke in. 'Even Gismond Brenley is a father first, whatever his business ethics are.' Inigo's rarefied world was showing itself in his assumptions.

'You would be wrong there. My father encouraged it. If needed, he'd say, we could blackmail someone with it later. No upstanding gentleman wanted to be labelled a debaucher of young girls.'

She saw Inigo's throat work as he swallowed. She'd managed to startle him. 'No one should grow up like that, Aud, to be made a whore by one's own father.'

'Not a whore in truth. I never lay with anyone,' she was quick to counter. She'd lain awake nights repeating that to herself. It had been her solace, that a part of her still remained clean and untouched. At least her father had understood the value of a maidenhead for the type of marriage he wanted to acquire for her.

Inigo reached for her hand where it lay in her lap. 'You will never have to do such a thing again, Aud.'

'I know, Inigo. That's why I came to you.' They were nearly to their evening stopping point. Signs of civilisation were visible in the rain outside the carriage windows. Good. She needed fresh air and some distance following her admission.

An afternoon of disclosures had left her emotionally exposed, her feelings raw and dangerous. She'd not meant to tell Inigo so much, but once she'd started, she couldn't seem to stop. She'd wanted him to know. Perhaps now he would understand better her reasons for making a clean break of things. But watching his face, feeling the press of his hand on hers in solidarity, conjured up a host of other feelings that transcended the tenuous friendship they'd begun. Yesterday, he'd been her hero. Today, he'd been her confidant and her confessor. Would he be more if she asked? A lover? A man she could trust not only with her secrets, but with her body as well? How wondrous it would be to have such a man, such an experience, if only once. It would be something to take into the void with her when she disappeared to hold against years of lonely freedom.

Chapter Twelve

She was alone and unprotected in the world. And she was counting on him. Inigo's mind kept going back to this over dinner. She was looking to him to protect her, at least until she could protect herself. Her story this afternoon had tugged at every notion of honour and chivalry he possessed. That a child should be treated as she'd been treated, manipulated to offer favours to men so that her father could benefit financially… It was a horrible evil, insidious in nature because she blamed herself for it. Even now, in the peace of the private parlour, Inigo wanted to run a rapier through Gismond Brenley for what he'd done to his daughter.

This afternoon had changed things between them. His anger at Brenley was now on Audevere's behalf. He wanted to fight for her. This was no longer about wanting justice for a dead friend or for those who'd been wronged by Brenley. It was intensely personal now in a way it hadn't been before. He wanted justice for a living, breathing woman who could still be saved, unlike Collin.

Inigo sliced the remainder of the bread. 'More?' He offered Audevere the plate. The firelight of the private parlour did her all kinds of favours, casting her features in soft light, catching the gold streaks in her blonde hair. The intimacy between them in the carriage lingered here over dinner. Did she feel it, too? That they were becoming something more than they had been? Two people hurtling towards some as yet undefined conclusion.

She shook her head. 'No, thank you. I've had enough. The stew was very good.' She drew a breath, a little nervous. 'We had a good first day. Do you think we were followed?'

They'd not talked of the journey itself, but perhaps it was time they did. He only had a few days to win her over. 'I don't think we were followed. The servants would have sent word by now to your father in Dover. He won't be back in London until tomorrow at the earliest. That will give us a two-day head start on him. If he decides to pursue directly.' Inigo thought that would not be the case. The threat posed by his letter would keep Brenley from rushing after them.

'A head start to where? I don't think we've established yet where we're going.' Audevere poured the remainder of the wine into his glass with a little smile that sent a shot of desire through him, his mind imagining her making that wifely gesture at their own dinner table, imagining her as his always. How could he not imagine such things after this afternoon? After listening to her story, after acknowledging how alone she was, how much she was depending on him whether she wanted to or not? The knight in him was left wanting to protect her while the primal man in him wanted to possess her, to claim her for all time so that no one could hurt her again. What would she say to that?

'To Boscastle, Aud. If you won't let me take you to Devonshire, then I will take you where you can be safe. I am taking you home.' Home, where she'd be surrounded by the love of his family. Home, where his strength lay: his father, Eaton and Eliza, the Trelevens and the Kittos. They would all rally around him—and her—once they understood the situation. And if he should fall, they would fight in his place to see Audevere safe.

The answer did not bring her the same peace it brought him. 'You cannot take me there,' she scolded, two bright spots of colour flushing her cheeks. 'They blame me for Collin's death. They will think I am beneath them, as you once did. Besides, I doubt your family would welcome the girl who jilted Collin Truscott. That *is* how the Cornish Dukes function, isn't it? All for one?'

'They will understand. We will explain everything,' Inigo assured her. He would make certain of it. 'I can think of nowhere better to go.'

'My father will know we're there. It's the first place he will look. He will come after us. It will make running away pointless,' she argued. 'The whole idea was to disappear and now, with that letter, he'll know exactly where I am and who I am with. There is no secrecy left, no escape.'

'That letter means we can end this. You won't have to live in fear of discovery the rest of your days. I do not want that for you if it can be avoided. Have you thought of what looking over your shoulder the rest of your life means?' She could not entangle a husband or children in that web of worry. Discovery would tear a family apart. No country squire, no village merchant or gentleman farmer would want to find out his wife had lied to him. Nor would they be up to the task of defending her—or themselves—against Brenley when he came. Fleeing, leaving her children behind, would destroy her.

'Never to know love? To have a family? Friends? Yes. I have thought of that, Inigo. I can have nothing but freedom and anonymity. It is the only choice I have if I want to be away from him.'

Inigo's frustration lifted its head. 'You're being stubborn, Aud. If you would give my plan a chance to work, you could have a real life.' They were starting to quarrel, giving their quiet new intimacy a sharp edge reminiscent of who they used to be. Perhaps they were both doing it on purpose. There was less temptation that way. He didn't want to want her, yet after today the want was more intense than ever.

* * *

'A real life? What do you suppose that is?' her reply softly mocked. Inigo's idea of a real life was a fairy tale. She could not allow that fantasy to take root for either of them. Perhaps most of all for herself. How much easier it would be to believe him, that such freedom and choice were possible, that she could have a man, love a man, like Inigo Vellanoweth and not ruin him, not rain down destruction on everyone and everything he held dear. If she gave in even a little to such a vision, they would both be lost. It took all her courage to meet his gaze, blue and intense across the little table. The earlier thought from the carriage played through her mind. She wanted him, this man who would defy the world for her. But there was risk in the wanting.

In this cosy, firelit room, the realisation both thrilled her and frightened her. He would become her lover if she asked, she was sure of it. Temptation flickered in his blue depths and it thrilled her. But claiming that thrill would mean something entirely different to him than it did to her. He would never let her leave and, in doing so, he would drag himself down, weighted by her secrets. Secrets that only had the power to hurt *if* she stayed, if she remained Audevere Brenley. Secrets that Inigo's letter to the King couldn't stop or change.

'All we have is now. There is no "real life" for us.' She made her case gently, aware that they sat on the edge of a quarrel, a conversation that perched on precarious old truths about a past they couldn't easily talk about. 'What do you think happens after Boscastle? Even if we speculate that everything is settled satisfactorily with my father, what happens then? I go back into society? I think not. I can *never* go back, Inigo. All I have left of this particular life is the next few days.' And in those days she wanted him. She let him see it in her eyes. He was not the only one who had suppressed desires. The difference was that she was willing to admit to them, to own them in full.

Inigo rose from the table, his face suddenly thunderous. 'I am sorry, Audevere. I cannot give you what you want.'

'You, Inigo. I want you and you are not oblivious to that or to wanting me.' Audevere rose to meet him, her restraint breaking. She'd not mistaken his desire, only his eagerness to deny it and it angered her. 'You once thought I was too low for Collin.' Her anger bubbled close to the surface. 'Am I still too low for you?'

'I was wrong to have said that.' Inigo was all quiet stoicism, his face a blank mask in his stiffness.

Audevere came around the table, her temper flaring. She wanted nothing more in the moment than to jar him out of his careful neutrality, to expose it for the weak façade it was. It did not fool her. 'Why not admit you have feelings for me that go beyond admiration?'

'Audevere, please. You are alone and perhaps

more frightened by that realisation than you're willing to admit. It's natural to want to reach out to someone at a time like this. We've had a long day and perhaps too much wine.' He was giving her every excuse, every possible chance to retract her boldness.

But Audevere pressed on. She was making him uncomfortable and that intrigued her. It meant she might be close to…something…something he didn't want her to see. What could he be hiding? A man like Inigo didn't have secrets. 'Perhaps I've had just enough wine to see things clearly.'

'What is it that you'd like to see? To know? This?' There was the slightest flair to his nostrils, the smallest of warnings that his cool reserve had broken momentarily before his hand grabbed her about the waist and dragged her to him, his mouth stopping hers with a reckless kiss, bruising in its intensity, savage in its possession. But it did not stun her, or stop her. This was what she'd asked for, this was what she'd wanted to know: what would it be like to kiss Inigo. To feel all that passion, all that intensity, bottled up inside him channelled into a single moment.

She answered with a fierceness of her own, her teeth sinking into his bottom lip, ferocious and hungry. She sensed she was both the challenged and the challenger in this wicked game, her own mouth begging him not to relent. His hands were in her hair, tangling in the thickness of her tresses, pins scattering on the ground as he bore her back against the wall, a gasp escaping as her back met with panelling and the tenor of their kiss changed. The fierce onslaught of emotion became a slow duel, tongues feinting, testing—a lunge here, a parry there. He was all skill and seduction, leading them on a passionate chase.

She was entirely aware of the press of his body, warm from the fire, from the heat of anger and newly roused passion slipped of its leash. The last sent a wave of desire cresting through her so thorough in its intensity it begged the question—how long had this intensity lain banked? How long had he wanted to hold her, feel her against him, drink from her mouth and to know that she wanted the same? To drink from him? How long had he dared to fantasise that she might respond in kind, not compelled by the rules of a silly party game? How long had he resisted the pull of the passion that devoured them now?

Her hands worked the knot of his neckcloth, their breathing coming hard, bodies melding together, hardness to softness, curve to muscled contour, against an inn wall in the middle of nowhere England, halfway between the past and the future. Inigo dragged his mouth from hers. 'I will not take you against a wall in a fit of desire.' His eyes blazed, his own breathing ragged, a testament to how much the effort cost him. No. There would be no talking him out of it. He was not that sort of man. The need to resist was there in his eyes as well.

'I must beg your pardon,' Inigo said, calling

on centuries of Boscastle breeding to see his way through this retreat. 'This was not well done of me.'

The leash was firmly back on his passions, but not before Audevere saw something else in those eyes as well. Guilt.

The question came again. *How long had he wanted this? How long had he fought this attraction?* A thought flickered through her mind, slipping away before she could hold on to it.

'Excuse me, I need to consult with the coachman.' Inigo made a short bow, a complete master of himself as if the moment had not happened. Of course he wouldn't want to stay in the parlour now. The thought came again, and this time, in the still of the parlour, she held on to it. He'd wanted her for years. He'd wanted her before Collin had died. His honour would be shamed by that. She pressed her fingers to her lips. Dear lord, what had she done? In a single kiss, she'd forced him to confess his darkest secret, something he'd hidden for years. Her own self-loathing swept her. What had she done to a good man? The old doubts returned in a rush: perhaps there was no good in her after all. And this time, there had been no push from her father. She and she alone had done it. She needed to make this right. Today, he'd offered her absolution in the carriage. Perhaps she could do the same for him.

Chapter Thirteen

She was waiting in his room when he came up the stairs, her hair unbound, her profile catching the lamplight. His gut tightened at the sight of her. How much torture did she think he could stand? Why couldn't she scurry off to hide like a sensible virgin after that display downstairs? He'd nearly had her up against a wall, for heaven's sake, in the parlour of a coaching inn! If she wasn't safe there where anyone could walk in, how did she imagine she'd be safe in his room where they would not disturbed?

'You shouldn't be here.' His tone was gruff. Her hair was down, her lips puffy. He was hard with the wanting of her, his trip outside in the cold having done nothing to alleviate the ache.

'How could I sleep after a kiss like that?' She ignored him. 'You are full of surprises, Inigo. All these years I thought you didn't like me. But that wasn't true.' She didn't even bother to ask it as a question. He'd hidden nothing tonight and it had backfired on him. It had not driven her away, had not repulsed her. It had only drawn her in.

'If you have it all worked out, why are you here?' Perhaps rudeness was his best defence, his best chance of getting her out of his room before he embarrassed them both. Perhaps she would do him the courtesy of not mentioning his greatest and guiltiest secret, which she had unmasked.

She rose and came to him. 'Because I hurt you tonight and I didn't mean to. In my own way, I forced a confession you didn't want to make. Can you forgive me?' She reached for his hand, but he stepped back. If she touched him, he would be lost.

He shrugged out of his jacket. He needed to keep himself busy. He did not want to look at her, did not want her to see any more than she already did. 'You're not the one in need of forgiveness.'

'Neither are you. There is nothing to forgive.' She persisted in following him about the room.

'Nothing to forgive?' He turned on her sharply, intending his words to shock. Bald-faced truth was usually an effective weapon against cajolery. 'I coveted my best friend's fiancée.'

She didn't give him a dratted inch. 'And you did not act on it. What could be more honourable and loyal than that? You did nothing to be ashamed of; you did not put your desires above your friendship with Collin and you certainly did not wish him death. There is no such thing.' She was making him out to be a saint. 'You are so much better than I.' She reached up a cool hand and stroked his hot cheek. 'Shall I tell you a secret? It's been five years and I can hardly remember his face. Soon, I won't remember him at all,' she said softly. 'I was supposed to marry him, supposed to love him until death do us part. And now I can't remember his face, the feel of his arms, nothing.'

'You were young—' Inigo said, but she cut him off.

'No, I do not get absolution if you will not grant it to yourself as well. What is your guilt, Inigo? That you lived? That you get to be here now? Collin would have wanted you to help me.'

'But not, perhaps, to bed you.' The words were out of his mouth before he could take them back. They were harsh and honest. This woman had him tied in knots, a man who invested huge sums of money calmly, who approached most of life with a cool detachment, who knew the rules and played by them without question.

'Why not if that's you want, what I want too?' She levelled her green gaze on him and he felt his resolve slip in the wake of her arguments. Why was he resisting indeed? 'Inigo, the past is buried, the future is uncertain. All we have is now.' She let a smile play across her lips, a smile that asked him to break all his rules, to set aside the self-imposed guilt he'd been carrying since Collin's death. Her voice dropped, low and smoky. 'You feel it, too. You kiss like a lit powder keg, all fireworks and explosions, like it's the last night of the world. And in your heart you know you are not far wrong. There is only now and the days before we reach Boscastle. We are guaranteed nothing beyond that.' She licked her lips. 'I know what I want. I want you to be my lover in the time that remains. I want you to kiss me again like the whole world is on fire and this time I don't want you to stop.'

He wanted that, too; his body ached with the wanting of it, even if the logic of it confounded his mind. At her words, the sum of the world shrank to the space of the small room. Nothing outside these walls mattered. All that mattered was to burn with her. To burn away the past, to cleanse himself of the guilt. His blood was already roaring with it. Fire was the great purifier. He shrugged out of his waistcoat. He would not disappoint her by pretending he did not understand what she asked, what she wanted: to burn away her past as well, to burn away the hands and mouths of men who had no claim to her, no right to her, but who had touched her anyway. She wanted to make love with a good man, an honourable man whom she could trust with this invitation. He was to be her crucible, the place where she could burn away all her impurities. And perhaps, in return, she could be his.

Inigo kissed her, his mouth firm and insistent in its acceptance. He drew her to her feet, his hands covering hers where they lay at the sash of her robe. 'Allow me. Let me do it,' he breathed. He would reveal her, unwrap her like the most precious of gifts. He untied the sash and pushed the robe from her shoulders, letting it fall to the floor in a pool of silk. The lamplight framed her from behind and his breath caught at the sight of the form revealed in the long silk slip she wore. The garment itself had been tailored simply and exquisitely, unadorned by ruffles and tucks or even ribbon. Its only adornment was the body that wore it. High, firm breasts, unaffected by corsetry, rose beneath the silk, the press of their peaks evident against the fabric while the material spilled over the round curve of her hips and the narrow line of her waist, the flat plateau of her belly.

His hands slid beneath the thin straps at her shoulders, taking them down one by one, until her breasts were revealed, then her stomach, her hips, and the silk fell away to join its partner on the floor. 'You're beautiful, Aud.' His voice was hoarse, his throat dry and the words did not do her justice. She was exquisite, beyond words, a goddess with her golden hair, her smooth porcelain skin, the silhouette of her body limned by the flame, the shadow between her legs dark, mysterious and inviting.

'Now you,' Audevere breathed. 'I want to see you. All of you.' She slid on to the big bed and curled on her side, ready to watch. He could not recall ever being studied so intently. His mistresses had undressed him, made wicked games out of it, but this was not like that. She was asking him to reveal himself, piece by piece, much like they'd revealed themselves to one another in the coach with their stories.

He divested himself of the waistcoat she'd undone, his fingers working the buttons of his shirt, pulling the tails free from his waistband. He watched her eyes go wide at the sight of his bare chest, watched her gaze drop as he pulled off his boots and worked loose the fall of his trousers, letting them slide down narrow hips, leaving him in his smallclothes. His arousal was blatantly evident, but he would not be ashamed of it. He desired her and he wanted her to know it beyond mere words. He saw her eyes rivet on the core of him as he finally stood before her, naked.

Dear heavens, he was magnificent! A god of old come to life as the clothes fell away from him, revealing sculpted muscle limning the smooth expanse of his chest, her eyes following down the lean hips to the long thighs of a fencer. Here was a man who took care of himself, who did not indulge in the dissipations offered by a life of luxury. At his groin, he rose, hard and powerful, a fitting match for the rest of him. Her hand reached out involuntarily as if she could stroke him at this distance. 'Come to bed, I want to touch you.'

'And *I* want to touch *you*.' The words were framed around a growl that sent the hairs on her arms prickling in delighted anticipation. The bed took his weight and Inigo settled beside her, a hand warm and flat on her belly as his mouth sought hers.

He did not merely touch her, he *worshipped* her. His hands, his words, his mouth, left no inch of her unexplored and Audevere revelled in it, in the sensation of being adored. He sucked at her breasts, his tongue laving each tip. He trailed kisses down the length of her to her belly, his hands framing her hips. He kissed her softly there, blowing a soft warm breath against her skin, then his mouth was at the nest of her, his hands spreading her legs, his thumbs massaging the insides of her thighs, and she opened for him. Her body cried out, *this* was what she wanted, his hands on her, his mouth on her until her core was shaking. His finger ran up the seam of her and a little mewl escaped her. She felt him shudder in answer and she understood implicitly that her pleasure wrought his. It pleased him to please her. How wondrous that realisation was. That true lovers sought to pleasure one another jointly and intimately.

He licked, his tongue following the track of his finger, then he looked up at her from the cradle of her thighs, his blue eyes burning. 'Do you like that, Aud?'

'Yes.' She could barely manage the one-word response. He bent to her pleasure again, his tongue finding the nub nestled deep in her folds, and licked at it until her mewls became gasps and her hands gripped his head for purchase as pressure built inside her like a wave that crested and ebbed and then crested again until Inigo brought the wave to a final crashing conclusion.

She was languid after that, floating in the aftermath of pleasure as Inigo gathered her to him, nuzzling her hair. 'That was extraordinary. I haven't any words for it,' she murmured. 'I had no idea a person could feel like that.'

'We are just getting started.' Inigo gave a hoarse laugh. 'There's more to come.'

'I should hope so.' Her hand slid between them, finding him strong and hard. She closed her hand about him, hearing the sharp intake of his breath. 'I want to touch you; it's only fair,' she argued softly.

To his credit, he did let her play a bit, explore the length of him. And she revelled in it—the smooth feel of his tip, the absolute hardness of him. 'Does it hurt?' she asked.

'Only if nothing is done about it.' Inigo laughed and rolled her beneath him. 'But seeing as I plan to do something about it, it's more of a dilettante's ache.' He fitted her beneath him, pressing himself at her entrance. Even then, his concern was for her. 'Are you sure, Audevere? There is nothing done yet.'

She looked up at him, her hands framing his face. 'I have never been more sure of anything or anyone in my entire life. I want this night, Inigo, and I want you.' She opened to him, giving him entrance, knowing full well that once done, this night could not be undone, what she gave him could not be ungiven. But this was her decision entirely, perhaps the first one that ever was.

He was gentle with her, skilled enough to know

what they both needed and disciplined enough to give it gently. Their joining was one of slow advancement and retreat as he accustomed her body to his, his strokes becoming longer, as he slid more easily, slid deeper into her. It was a tantalising, intimate progress that teased her with an echo of earlier pleasure. There was a tender part of her that seemed to weep for him, crying out every time he passed over it, until the fleeting pleasure of that notice was not enough to satisfy her. Audevere arched her hips against him, wanting to claim more of that pleasure. Her breaths came in begging pants now, her legs wrapped about his lean hips, wanting to hold him captive, wanting to hold him accountable for rendering the pleasure complete. She would not let him leave her until the pleasure was done.

He sensed the urgency, the desire, his own breaths coming in ragged inhalations now, the speed of his thrusts accelerating in tandem with the cries of her body, perhaps even as excited by them as she was. Her hands gripped his shoulders as the pleasure swelled, threatening to sweep her away. In the end, she let it have its way with her, let it sweep over her and carry her out to the depths of pleasure's seas. She did not care where it took her as long as Inigo was there, her one anchor. And Inigo *was* with her, right up until the end, his own pleasure coming apace with hers, withdrawing only as she crested one last time to make a gentleman's finish in the sheets. Honourable until the last. She had no doubts as to the discipline such a consideration demanded from a man.

She was truly spent now, entirely boneless as she floated in pleasure's quieter seas now. So this was lovemaking; this was true pleasure. Now she knew and she was glad for it. The experience had not disappointed. How sad, though, that she might never have it again, that she might never have *him* again. She was not naive enough to think she could recreate these sensations with just any man. Tonight was the product of far more than two people seeking pleasure. Tonight was because of Inigo.

The fire in her banked a bit, satisfied for the moment that the flames had done their job. She was at peace, Inigo's arms about her, the world beyond this room obliterated. In these precious, quiet moments of absolute tranquillity, nothing else mattered and everything was possible. She let out a drowsy sigh, her head pillowed against the muscle of Inigo's chest. The world could not touch them tonight. They were beyond it, in a place of their own.

Chapter Fourteen

Silly girl. Did she think she could outrun him? Out-wit him? Had she not learned there was no place she could hide? Gismond Brenley crushed the letter in his hand, grinding it in unrestrained anger. This was not the triumphant homecoming he'd imagined when he'd left for Dover, on the brink of claiming Trem-blay's favour at last. But now, he'd been summoned home early, no proposal in hand, to find his daugh-ter gone, run off with the very man who threatened to steal all he'd worked for.

Brenley's temper flared again. How dare Inigo Vellanoweth threaten to have his title stripped? How dare he threaten to go to the King? Oh, he knew very well how the man dared it. There was little to fight Tintagel with. Dealing with Tintagel and the Cor-nish Dukes was different from dealing with regular men. Gismond had learned that last year during the situation with the Blaxford mines. He'd distributed a defamatory pamphlet to discredit Eliza Blaxland's leadership of the mining conglomerate, only to discover that pamphlets might influence small folk, but they did not influence or stop the might of the Cornish Dukes. Inigo had simply ignored the pamphlet and arranged to have the mining board bought out, old members supplanted with those who would pay no heed to the rumours. Then Lynford had gone and married the chit and put her above any attempt at scandal.

Gismond tapped his long fingers on the desk in an irritated tattoo. There would be scandal aplenty this time, though. Inigo had upended his plans and attacked his hard-won social standing. There would be no marriage to Viscount Tremblay now. Tremblay would hardly want a bride who'd run off with another man let alone offer business opportunities to her father. The whole trip to Dover was now a complete waste. Had it ever actually been within his grasp? Brenley was starting to wonder now, a fresh wave of anger surging. Perhaps Tremblay had been brought in on it, a decoy to lure him out of town so Inigo and Audevere—he couldn't discount his daughter's role in all this—could act.

Vellanoweth had conspired against him on all fronts: financially, socially, and personally. He'd gone too far this time and it would bring him down. Brenley could not let this go unchecked. To do so would be to validate the threat. He didn't doubt Vellanoweth would follow through either. One wrong move and he would make his case to the King. Brenley knew how that would turn out. The King loved the money he made for the coffers, but he loved the Cornish Dukes more. He would not risk offending them by siding with Brenley.

Brenley gave orders he was not to be disturbed and shut himself away to think. Vellanoweth had to be stopped. Quite often the key to stopping a man lay in his motives. Take away his motives and a man seldom had a reason to risk anything. He poured a drink and settled into his favourite chair by the fire. What motivated Vellanoweth?

Was this still about avenging that silly, weak boy, Collin Truscott, or was this about Audevere? Did Vellanoweth fancy himself in love with her? He wouldn't be the first man to fall for her charms. Were they lovers? Business partners? Had he convinced her or had she convinced him? The latter seemed more likely, assuming Audevere had worked up the courage. He'd known his daughter was angry with him for some time. But he'd not imagined she'd have the fortitude to actually leave. Was she really willing to leave behind the luxury, the social standing, her reputation? True, he had made her work for those luxuries, but how else did she think to attain such comfort? Surely she understood running away meant embracing a life of limited means and poverty. She would never again live as she'd lived under his roof. And she couldn't keep her name or else her secret would find her, *he* would find her. Unless…

Unless Tintagel had convinced her she could ac-

tually escape him without giving up all that. In order
to get those promises though, she'd need to persuade
him to fall in love with her first. The Cornish Dukes
put much stock in the concept of love. They were
known for their love-matches and thus far their heirs
had made an awful habit of repeating those mistakes: Lynford with Eliza Blaxland and Trevethow
with Lady Penrose. If Audevere was smart, she'd seduce Tintagel and then extract all nature of promises
from him, starting with marriage. That could work in
Audevere's favour, but it wouldn't change anything
and it certainly wouldn't stop him.

The joke would be on Vellanoweth. If he married her, she'd bring him down. Brenley chuckled to
himself. Audevere's beauty was her only asset. She
was a ticking time bomb waiting to go off, her very
own worst enemy. How would Tintagel react once
he knew the truth about Audevere's birth? The real
question was when to tell him: before the marriage or
after. Which would be the most devastating? Which
would offer the greatest opportunity for blackmail?

While all that would be sweet revenge, it did not
resolve the larger issue of protecting his title and his
status. If he didn't marry her, if she was to be his
lover but not his wife or if he had only spirited her
away for financial gain or for revenge, Tintagel's
threat remained dangerous. He needed to make Vellanoweth look like the villain in this piece.

A few strategies came to mind. First, he could
spread rumours that Tintagel had stolen his daugh-

ter and publicly demand honour be satisfied. That was the best gambit: to force Tintagel into marriage with her. Even now, her chastity would be in question. She'd been alone on the road with a man for days. He could paint quite a defamatory picture of Tintagel: the man who'd absconded with his dead best friend's former fiancée, stealing her from her father's home while her father was out of town on business and then been alone with her for days.

Brenley chuckled to himself. He quite liked the idea of making Vellanoweth look like a bride stealer. He also liked the idea of appearing as the wronged father. A duchess as a daughter would be delightful. It would force Tintagel to give him entrance into the circle of the Cornish Dukes. By fighting him, Tintagel actually ended up giving him everything he'd ever wanted. He could already see Cassian Truscott's face when he came home from honeymooning, could already imagine the looks on the Duke of Bude's and the Duke of Hayle's faces when they had to greet him as an equal, as *family*. Nothing mattered more to those Dukes than family and now their nemesis would be part of theirs.

Brenley pulled out his stationery and began to write. He'd see what Inigo Vellanoweth made of that. Marry his daughter or else… The 'or else' part was a bit ambiguous. Refusing to marry Audevere gave Brenley every right to act the aggrieved parent. He could defame Tintagel, but then Tintagel might go to the King anyway. That had to be prevented at all costs. He had men who could see to that, although he'd rather have the satisfaction himself. He smiled coldly to himself. A duel wouldn't be amiss. Sanctioned murder among gentlemen. He'd shoot the bastard and put an end to his interference once and for all. It wouldn't be as lucrative as marriage, but it would be a lot more decisive. Well, he'd be magnanimous and let Tintagel choose: marriage or death. Meanwhile, he'd slowly make his way to Truro and await Tintagel's answer there.

She had died and gone to heaven. Audevere stretched, her body and her mind reluctant to leave the peace of half-sleep, both replete with memories of the night before. Inigo had been an exquisite lover, gentle and passionate by turn, matching his prowess to her need. She was pleasantly sore, memories of last night returning to her now in the early dawn: the skill of his mouth, the ability of his body to exact every ounce of pleasure from hers.

No, not *exacting*. Her mind stumbled over the word. Exacting described what other men had taken from her. It suggested that Inigo had claimed by force what she'd offered freely. To recall his passion was to recall her own. She'd not dreamed such pleasure was possible. Her own response had equalled his in all ways. Such a consuming, uncontrollable response was entirely new to her. Collin's kisses, Tremblay's kisses, and certainly not the advances made by her father's so-called friends had ever elicited such a reaction from her. It was something she wanted to feel again. Perhaps that made her wanton. At the moment, she didn't care. She was sleepy, safe and warm with Inigo's arm draped about her, protectively, and perhaps possessively, too. A man like him would be. A woman could get used to being loved by such a man. He had handled everything with such ease and elegance: the lap robes, the picnic basket, the stops along the way to stretch her legs, the speed with which dinner had been served and a private parlour arranged.

She snuggled down into the blankets, her buttocks wiggling against Inigo's groin, his length stirring against her in response. He murmured, coming awake, his arm tightening around her, drawing her close against him as he took her into the curve of his body. It was an intimate reminder that the confessions of yesterday and the acts of last night had altered her lens of understanding everything between them. This relationship was no longer a partnership focused on her escape, or on merely bringing down her father. This was now a partnership in which she and Inigo harboured unexplored passions for one another. Last night had been only the start of that exploration, but it raised the question: did they dare go further? Was it enough that curiosity had been slaked? She didn't believe for a moment last night had been about curiosity, though. It had been about purging guilt, about confession and absolution, about putting the past behind them, about starting over with a clean slate. Hadn't they both needed to know they were worthy of happiness? Deserving of love no matter how fleeting? Whatever had been put to bed last night, it didn't change the future. She still had to disappear.

Inigo's mouth tugged gently at her earlobe and she gave the thought up for later. It was far more pleasant to think of the present when it involved being buried beneath quilts, Inigo taking her with tantalising slowness from behind, his hands at her breasts, his mouth at her ear whispering decadent promises she couldn't let him keep as he drove her wild, pushing her relentlessly towards full waking. But oh, what a delicious way to awake.

She knew intuitively this was how mornings should always begin. Just as she knew that autumn afternoons should involve a carriage ride on dry roads, a roadside picnic, followed by a walk beneath the crimson leaves of an oak grove turned shades of red and russet and vermilion in one last burst of glory before winter.

'When we were growing up, Eaton's father would take us truffle hunting in the Trevaylor Woods.' Inigo regaled her with stories of his childhood in Cornwall, how Eaton's father had taught them to cook out of doors over a fire, how Eaton's hound was a special breed of dog who could smell truffles, how he and his friends would spend the autumn nights sleeping beneath the autumn sky, the stars bright against the darkness. 'We'd stay up half the night looking at constellations.' Inigo laughed and she laughed with him.

She hugged his arm tight as they walked. 'I like you this way, happy and laughing.' She'd liked it so much there'd been times today when she'd forgotten to worry about her father, about where they were going, about what she would do once she got there, what the rest of her life would look like once she cut this last final tie. Perhaps that was why he'd been so entertaining. Maybe he was also trying to forget the things that lay ahead. In the forgetting about the past and the future, they could enjoy the present.

Audevere slid him a sidelong glance from beneath the brim of her bonnet, taking in the strong, stark planes of his face, and the firm mouth that was curved up in a rare smile. He was turned out today in the same clothes he'd worn yesterday, as was she. Audevere gave a little laugh. 'How simple life can suddenly be. Here we are, wearing the same clothes as yesterday, miles from civilisation, miles from any sophisticated entertainments to keep us busy, and I'm happier than I've ever been.' It was true. She didn't need cupboards full of gowns, or invitations piled up in the hall. She just needed this: the peace of walking in nature, talking with a friend, distance from the life she'd led in London, distance from her father. Or, her mind prompted, was it that she just needed him? Inigo. Was it the distance that brought her the happiness she felt today, or was it the man beside her? If it was the distance, she could have that always. That was what escaping her father had been about. But if it was the man, she would lose him. She could have this only for a little while, just like the brilliance of the leaves.

'I'm glad, Aud. You deserve to be happy,' Inigo's hand covered hers where it lay on his sleeve as he turned them back towards the coach. There were still miles to cover before they reached their destination tonight. Yet she would delay their return for a little longer.

'As do you.' She gave him a small smile. 'Do I make you happy, Inigo?' Had last night meant as much to him as it had to her? Among the many things they'd not discussed today was last night. Here was a man who'd carried feelings for her, hidden away for so many years, and yet last night he'd served her, worshipped her, put her before the claiming of his own pleasure, the fulfilment of his own fantasies. 'Did I disappoint you?

Inigo frowned, his brow furrowing. 'Whatever gave you that idea? Of course not. Aud, how could you ever disappoint me? I've waited for you for so long. I've vacillated between wanting you, giving you up, hating myself for the wanting, convincing myself I didn't want you, couldn't want you, and then, just when I thought I was safe, there you were on the Bradfords' veranda in that cranberry silk and the wanting started all over again…and the doubt, and the misery of being trapped between the two, and I knew I'd never be safe from you.'

The woods were silent, as she stood beneath the trees in awe, overwhelmed by his confession. But, of course, Inigo was always intense, the very personification of still waters running deep, so deep that she might drown in them. How easy it would be to let go and allow the current of Inigo's words to take her away from her resolve for a new life, a new name. 'And now?' she whispered. 'Are you safe from me now?' Perhaps now that his fantasy was fulfilled, the sharp edge of desire would be dulled. Men were like that. They loved the hunt, but once the prize was caught, they quickly lost interest.

'I don't want to be safe, Aud. I want to be with you. To show you—'

She pressed a finger to his lips. She didn't want to hear what he might show her for fear they would argue over it. She could guess very well what those things might be and how much she wanted them, too.

'I don't want to be safe either,' Audevere breathed her own fantasy to life, the one that had been seeded this morning in his arms and had put down roots throughout the day with every glance, every story, every touch. She wanted to seize these days of pleasure and hold them against all the lonely days to come. If only he would grant them to her.

'I want to be like the leaves on the trees, Inigo. I want to burn my brightest just before I die.' A sensual smile played across her lips. She watched his eyes light with desire at her words. She would not wait for him to bring the fantasy to her. She would issue the invitation to him. 'I want to burn with you for however long we have. Will you burn with me, Inigo?'

'God, yes.' His voice was a husky rasp as he reached for her and lit the match.

Chapter Fifteen

Inigo took her mouth in a hard kiss, his body on fire at her words, her touch. The very sensuality of what she asked of him left him aroused and aching. He would take the invitation to be her lover. There was no dishonour in it. He would do more than burn with her. He would protect her, he would keep her safe always. She was his now even if she did not understand it yet. But she would. He had time. Two more precious days on the road to persuade her she didn't have to disappear, two days until they reached Boscastle, and she would see anew that he could offer her what she'd never had: the unconditional support of friends and family. She was not impressed by riches or elevated society. He would give her something far more valuable: his family, his name, his protection, his body, and his heart, if she would take them.

She gasped in excitement at the roughness of their kiss and answered with a fierceness of her own, her teeth sinking into his bottom lip as desire ignited, flaming to life between them. He pressed her back against the broad trunk of an oak, her hand dropping between them, seeking the hard root of him through his trousers. They were not being safe now, they were being reckless, letting passion consume them as it had last night, letting passion become an excuse for not looking ahead.

He lifted her then, taking her legs about his waist, her skirts falling back, helped by the rough sweep of his hand up her thighs. Her hands worked the fall of his trousers open, freeing him to thrum erect against her damp core. Her arms wound about his neck, her body pressed to his, her head tilted back, mouth open and pleasure purling in the back of her throat, a sensual mewl that set his blood afire with proof that she was burning, too, for him, for the possibility of all they could be together.

All else ceased to matter. He pushed away consequences and complications. For the first time in his life, *now* was all that mattered. It was heady and liberating. He claimed her in a swift thrust that wrenched a cry from them both and then the rhythm of taking and giving began, her hips hard against his, the intensity of the encounter driving them fast and furiously to pleasure's edge and over. This passion would be short-lived and explosive, but no less brilliant, no less powerful for its brevity. Climax swept them, Audevere's sharp cry breaking the silence of the woods and he buried his head against her shoulder as he spent himself, his own body sweat-slicked despite the cold, his breath coming in frosty pants as he set her down.

He felt her hand threading through his hair, 'I don't think I've ever seen you messy,' she laughed softly at his ear. 'Your shirt's untucked, your trousers askew, your hair mussed.'

'If I'm a mess, it's all your doing, minx.' Inigo teased, pressing a kiss to her throat.

Her arms wound around his neck. 'I like you messy, imperfect. It proves that Inigo Vellanoweth is human after all.' She smiled at him and he thought about the possibility of never leaving these woods. What he would give to stay here in this moment for ever.

He kissed her one last time, letting her taste reluctance on his tongue. 'Come, the horses will be waiting.' Then he took her by the hand and led her from the woods.

A walk in the bracing autumn air, and rather vigorous activity involving an oak tree combined with the rocking motion of the coach lulled Audevere to sleep before they'd gone far. But Inigo's mind was too awake to sleep, filled with the rash promises he'd made.

I will protect her. I will keep her safe. She is mine now.

Inigo looked down at the blonde head resting against his shoulder. He'd meant all of it. But how to deal with Brenley?

By now, Brenley would be home from Dover. He would have read the letter. Brenley would have understood the implications of moving against him, which meant Brenley would have come up with options. The man's business dealings were hydra-like. When one avenue was shut down, he merely found another until he got what he wanted. It was that tenacity which made Inigo's plan dangerous. Would Brenley come after him directly? Inigo thought of the duelling pistols beneath the seat. He was ready should that be the case. Would Brenley come after him indirectly? More hired thugs on a dark road? He was ready for that, too. Or was there another option that he'd yet to consider?

He didn't dare discuss it with Audevere. The more she had to worry about, the more likely it was she would try to run. *'I want to burn like the leaves before I die.'* She'd meant before she took a new name and disappeared from this life as she knew it. And she would definitely disappear if she thought resolving the situation with her father involved a duel. No argument he could make would be able to persuade her. Yet he would face that deadly risk for her. He could not lose her now. He'd taken her to bed, shown them both what could come of their passion and nothing he'd ever experienced with a lover came close to rivalling it. To lose her now would be to lose a part of himself.

Then what? How do you propose to keep her? The question was whispered. *Do you intend to marry her? What will your family think? What will your friends think? What will Cassian think when he comes home and sees that you've married his dead brother's fiancée?*

Cassian would come around as Vennor had, he told himself fiercely. As for what happened when they arrived at Boscastle, his family would give her sanctuary because he asked it of them. But in his heart, he knew their acceptance of her was important to him. They were his family, the people he loved and cared for most in this world. Surely they would see the woman he saw when he looked at her?

Audevere shifted against him. Perhaps the real reason he wanted their acceptance of her was that he wanted to give Audevere a family to replace to the one she'd never had. He could see her with them now like a Wilson landscape, four figures walking along the cliff path at Boscastle, little Ben holding her hand, the girls laughing. How long could such a vision last? He could give her that illusion of family for a few weeks, a few months, even as long as Christmas. Holidays at Boscastle were splendid, a celebration of family and love. But there would be questions as to the reasons she was there, scepticism from those who knew her history, perhaps even scandal. A man did not bring a woman home to the family pile, unchaperoned, without it meaning something; a visit home would be seen as a prelude to a proposal.

Of course he would ask. He would ask now if he thought there was any chance of her accepting. What happened if she still refused his proposal after being welcomed by his family? She might not wish to belong to any man after having just won her freedom from her father.

How could he dishonour her by keeping her as his mistress? It was protection of a sort, but he could not bring such a woman home to his family, could not offer anything more substantial beyond the sanctuary of the Devonshire cottage. His father would be furious with him for introducing her to the girls, for seating her at the same table as his sainted mother. And rightly so. He'd learned honour from his father. He did not want to have to choose between Audevere and his family. He wanted them to be one and the same.

His arm tightened around her at the thought of losing her. To keep her by marriage or to lose her for ever. Those seemed his only two choices and both of them tore at his heart. It seemed there were no easy choices. Was this how Cassian and Eaton had felt when they'd fallen in love with their wives? Had their minds been pits of turmoil, too? Had they seen what they wanted and then been hindered in the getting of it? He thought of some of the harsh, blunt advice he'd given them and now regretted it.

Audevere woke as the coach pulled into the inn. The last of the sun slanted in through the coach window, burnishing her hair to a platinum sheen, highlighting the pale perfection of her profile, and when she lifted those aventurine eyes, she stole his breath. Was there a more beautiful woman than Audevere?

She smiled self-consciously at his scrutiny. She raised a hand to her hair. 'I must look a fright, my hair is so tangled and my face is full of sleep.' She rubbed her cheek where his coat had left a crease on her skin.

'Not at all. I think you look quite wonderful.' Wonderfully ravished, if truth be told. He wasn't sure he wanted the taproom to get a look at her like this. 'Wait here for me while I see to our lodgings.' He opened the door and felt her hand at his sleeve, her voice low, private, just for him.

'Inigo, don't waste money on two rooms tonight.'

She was playing a dangerous game with herself. She knew very well that her reasons for indulging in this mad passion were not the same as Inigo's. She indulged because it couldn't last. But his honour would demand more than a three-day fling on the Great South-west Road. He would want to make good on those promises he whispered so intently in her ear as they made love—promises of protection, promises of a new life without giving up the old. And he would die for them if she stayed. How did she make him see that the threat of death was not an idle one? How did she make him see that he could not win this battle of wills with her father?

Audevere repinned her hair, each tangle reminding her of what had transpired beneath the autumn canopy in the woods. The mysterious, quiet, Inigo Vellanoweth of her youth was indeed a powder keg of a lover. It was a heady and addictive experience, one she would be loath to give up when the time came. He'd rescued her; he'd believed in her. He deserved more from her than to have his kindness repaid with death. He did not deserve to die for her any more than Collin had.

She was in over her head. This was not supposed to have happened. She had not counted on this depth of feeling on her part and certainly not on his when she'd asked for his help. She'd counted on his honour overriding his dislike. She'd not counted on his dislike being a ruse for his deeper desire. Nor had she counted on his kisses lighting her up like Vauxhall fireworks, leaving her breathless and wanting more. She'd thought she was done with men, that she'd had her fill, that she knew all there was to know about them. But she'd been wrong. There was one man she'd not known.

That man loves you. That man has waited all these years for you, battled his personal demons for you. He will not let you go so easily. He will want to fight for you because he thinks you're worth it. Her conscience whispered the awful truth. *You have to tell him you're not. Tell him the truth about your birth.*

Audevere pressed her hand to the pocket of her skirt, feeling the small, hard shapes she carried inside. In case she'd had to leave her valise behind in her attempt to escape the house, she'd wanted these two things with her. She'd not been willing to leave without them. She should show him, tell him the great secret that had kept her tethered to her father these past years and the secret that would ensure Inigo would let her disappear. It would show him how impossible any other option was.

The coach door opened, a gust of cold air blowing in with it. 'I've got our room, Mrs Vellanoweth.' Inigo's eyes held hers in meaningful congress that sent a rush of warm pleasure through her darker thoughts. Dear lord, he was irresistible, all commanding presence and elegance even after two days in the same clothes. She made the devil's own deal with herself. She would play his wife. She could have tonight and tomorrow. They would make no difference in the long run. But she promised herself she would tell him before they reached Boscastle and then she would leave, completing her escape alone if necessary, because she suspected she loved him too much not to.

Chapter Sixteen

Love was a strong word, an intense word, for a strong and intense man. But she could think of no word that served better to describe the emotions Inigo raised in her. From the least of his actions to the most intimate, she was falling in love with him. This was yet another unlooked-for consequence of this mad decision of hers to run away, Audevere thought as she studied her pretend husband in the carriage on the third day of their journey. She'd not expected to fall in love or even to establish an attachment. She'd warned herself against it that night at cards when the first threads of wanting had started to wind themselves tight about her. This was not the time.

That argument had not lasted long. This was exactly the time. She was about to disappear, to become someone else. Her virginity was of no consequence in that new life and her old life and old acquaintances would cease to matter.

She hazarded another glance at Inigo over the rim of her book. An affair was not as simply managed as she'd thought. Indulging in physical passion was one thing, something easily walked away from when the indulgence was over. But she was discovering that indulging in love was quite another. Love was not so easily walked away from.

'Is your book good?' Inigo drawled, looking up from his own reading. He caught her eyes and she saw in his gaze the echoes of a morning spent abed longer than usual. As a result, they had made a late start of it, promising themselves they would not stop for lunch in order to make Exeter by nightfall.

'Yes,' she offered the little lie and Inigo laughed.

'You promised me honesty, Aud. You haven't turned a single page since you started reading.'

She closed the book, marking her place with a finger. 'The book *might* be good. I just happened to find something else *more* interesting at the moment.' She gave him a saucy grin. 'Why would I want to read a book, when I could read you?' She set the book aside altogether now that she had his attention. Their time was so short. Tonight would be their last night on the road, in this beautiful time between where they answered to no one but themselves. They would have most of tomorrow in the carriage, but she knew by then the real world would start to intrude. Their thoughts would be occupied by their arrival and their reception. What would greet them at the end of this journey? Until then, she wanted to keep Inigo to herself a while longer, to learn as much as she could of this extraordinary man.

'Teach me a game, Inigo. What did you boys do to pass the time when you travelled to school?' She loved his stories, each one offering new insights into who he was and what had made him.

'All right.' Inigo grinned, something he'd done far more of on this trip than at any other time she'd known him. 'I will teach you to play pockets. It's a game the four of us made up. But,' he cautioned with mock sternness, 'you have to be honest and you cannot renege. There is no substitution for the truth. Here's how it works. I pick something from your pocket and you have to tell the story behind it. Then you can pick something from my pocket and I have to tell you.'

'You're assuming I have pockets, or that anything is in them,' Audevere prevaricated. She liked the idea of this game less when she thought about what she had in her skirt pocket. She wanted one last night before she told him her last and most damning secret.

'You do, I noticed them on your carriage ensemble this morning. You won't get out of this, Aud,' he teased and then softened his tone, reassuring her as always that he would protect her. 'It's just the two of us. No one needs to know what we say to one another in here.' He gestured to the confines of the carriage. 'This is our world for now. You are safe here.' His eyes dropped to her hip, to the pocket in her skirt where a soft impression was outlined. Inigo coaxed her with a slow, winning smile, 'Show me.'

Audevere drew out a packet of white tissue paper. She unwrapped it to reveal a length of wide, pink, silk ribbon, carefully folded and pressed. 'There's yards of it.' She held up an end where the ribbon had been cut. 'I left some of it for my maid, along with a note from me, thanking her for her service. I wish I could have left her more. I am sure she'll need money, but I had none to give her. My father will probably turn her out without a reference. He'll blame her even though she's entirely innocent.' She pleated the ribbon between her fingers. 'I left him to free myself from his dirty work and to save Tremblay the way I could not save Collin. But it still seems others will suffer, perhaps others who are less able to fend for themselves like Patsy.' She sighed. 'I just want it to end.'

Inigo reached across the carriage for her hand. 'It will. Soon all this will be over.'

Yes, it would be. But perhaps not in the way Inigo imagined.

'Why is it in your pocket?' Inigo prompted, returning them to the game.

'The ribbon is pretty and I like pretty things.' Audevere gave a soft laugh. 'I imagine I will have few pretty things in my future. This ribbon will remind me of what I gave up in order to be free, as well as the corruption that allowed me those luxuries, that my comfort was built on someone else's discomfort.'

'Where did it come from?' Inigo asked as she wrapped it up and returned it to her pocket.

'A dressmaker's box.' She blushed. The memory seemed silly now in light of all that had happened. 'It came with the gown I wore to the Bradfords' ball, the first night we talked. I was excited when the box came. But my father was quick to tell me the gown was meant to entice the Viscount back into our clutches. He'd meant for me to wear it for the announcement of my engagement. He did not shy away from letting me know I'd failed in that regard.' The ribbon was another symbol of why her escape was worth all the sacrifice, even the sacrifice of Inigo. She wrapped it up in the paper and slid it back into her pocket as if she could slide the memories back in there as well. Out of sight, out of mind. 'Your turn, Inigo. What's in your pocket? Although it hardly seems fair. You have so many pockets to choose from.'

He did. There were the deep pockets of his great-coat, the small, narrow pockets of his waistcoat, the inner pockets of his jacket. 'I wish women's clothes had as many pockets as men's.' She tossed her head. 'It's a form of oppression, you know. This is one of the subtle ways men keep women down. Pockets make your life portable. You can carry a pocket watch and all nature of useful items, all of them easily accessible on your person without the need to be hampered by a reticule. Between a reticule and managing one's skirts, it's no wonder we have to constantly take a man's arm while you have your hands free all the time.'

'The better to defend you with, my dear.' Inigo laughed at her spirited dissertation. 'How could I draw my sword or my pistol if I had a reticule of my own?'

'Precisely! What if I want to defend myself? How shall I draw *my* sword? *My* gun? *My* knife?'

'Have you ever needed to, Aud?' Inigo's teasing had faded to instant seriousness.

'There have been times when I've wanted to, even at the risk of earning my father's displeasure,' she said quietly. Some women made the argument about pockets as part of the new theories of feminism. But she made the argument for very practical reasons.

'Your father's men.' Inigo's tone was deadly. She watched his hand flex at his side.

'Yes. There was one man in particular I wouldn't have minded slicing. I did not think I was in any real danger. He'd brought me a box of bon-bons that evening. He strolled the room with me after dinner while the others played cards. I didn't think I was in any danger. But then we found ourselves in an alcove and he'd drawn the curtain.'

She didn't like remembering it. He'd kissed her there, by force after she'd declined. 'He said I owed him. He'd brought me gifts; surely I didn't think they came without expectations.' He'd done more than kiss her. He'd asked her to take down her dress and when she'd refused he'd ripped it. 'It was the first time I really saw how my father was using me. Before, I had not made the connection between the little favours and flattery. There'd only been a few harmless kisses at that point. I was too naive to see the connection.' She looked at Inigo. His features were drawn tight and he bristled on her behalf.

'Perhaps you should start a new fashion for ladies,' he said in all seriousness. 'You should have gowns with holsters built into them for those times when a man is not a gentleman, although I wish those times didn't exist, that such things were not needed.' They sat in silence, listening to the road, each reflecting on her story. 'Aud, you are safe with me. I would never make presumptions on your person.'

She smiled and said simply, 'I know.' He was careful with her in all ways: careful to leave her as he climaxed, careful to take his cues for lovemaking from her, letting her initiate, although he took over once she made her desire known. A man like Inigo could never relinquish control for long, which made his efforts all the more dear to her.

She expelled a breath. 'We've digressed. It's my turn to pick one of your myriad pockets.' Audevere bit her lower lip as she contemplated his person, letting her eyes rove over him, stopping now and then on a pocket. Her gaze returned to his midsection. 'That one. The little pocket on your waistcoat.'

'Are you sure you don't want to pick a bigger pocket?' Inigo encouraged. 'Perhaps I don't have anything in this pocket. It's so small.'

'The best things come in small packages, don't you know that?' Audevere laughed. 'I am sure. That's my choice, especially when I think you protest the choosing of it too much.' What kind of secret did the honourable Inigo Vellanoweth hide in his pocket? She was on the edge of her seat, suddenly filled with twin measures of intrigue and trepidation. Perhaps it was a token from a lover? Past or…present? Surely not present. Surely she'd not misjudged him. There was only her, but what if she was wrong? What if he had lied or she had somehow misunderstood? What if Inigo Vellanoweth wasn't any better than any other man in the end and she'd trusted with him the most important parts of her?

Every nerve, every thought was raw and waiting. She'd never felt more exposed than she did right now. But perhaps this was what happened when one threw caution to the wind. It was her fault. He'd hinted it was the pocket he'd least wanted her to choose, the pocket that exposed him the most.

She watched as Inigo unbuttoned the pocket and put in two fingers to retrieve the single item that resided there. He brought it out in a closed fist. She could not see it as he rolled it around in his hand, her mind running rampant through options. Was it a stone? A piece of jewellery? What might be so small and so meaningful? He held out his closed fist and opened it to reveal the ring sitting in the palm of his hand. The antique gold patina of the band caught the light, the square sapphire in its centre flamed with the sun. 'This is Richard Penlerick's ring,' he said, as if those words alone explained everything.

The dead Duke of Newlyn. One of the Cornish Dukes. Inigo's mentor. She knew without question when she looked upon that ring that she was looking upon Inigo's heart. The old expression of holding one's heart in one's hands took on new and literal meaning.

'May I?' Audevere asked. Perhaps he did not intend for her to touch it. He nodded and she gingerly held the ring up to study it, turning it towards the light. It was gold and heavy, elegant, expensive, a man's ring. But she did not think that was why Inigo treasured it. For a man who made money, he had a unique tendency to value sentiment over treasure: honour, love, loyalty, friendship. She tilted the ring. Inside the band there was script, tiny, neat. It looked like Latin. 'What does it say?' She offered the ring back to him.

'Ad honorem.' Inigo tucked it safely back into his pocket. 'For honour. Each of the four Dukes have a similar ring. The sapphire represents truth and loyalty, which are the pillars of honour.'

'He did not leave it for his son?' Audevere thought it odd that the ring had come to him and not the Duke's heir.

'The Duke gave it to me when I finished at Oxford, as a gift,' Inigo explained. 'I think he meant it as a talisman to ward off greed and avarice. I have a talent for making money. I think he meant this as a reminder to use that talent for the benefit of more than just myself. A reminder, too, to honour my family in all things. Money can be a dirty subject among peers. I am careful not to shame my family with my "dubious" talent.'

He gave a wry smile that made Audevere laugh as he continued. 'Peers are just supposed to *have* money and not know where it comes from. It's a naive attitude if you ask me. It's no wonder so many peerages are impoverished these days. So, I have discreet businesses and investment groups made up of other like-minded souls who don't expect their family fortunes to magically multiply in the dark.'

'Oh, I thought it had come to you after he died.' Audevere hesitated over each word, aware that she trod on difficult ground. The Duke's death had been sudden and violent. It had shaken London. She could only imagine how it had affected those closest to him.

'No, but his death certainly adds more meaning to the ring, a way to keep him close to me. He was a mentor to all of us, just as each of our fathers are.'

'You are very lucky.' Audevere was silent for a moment, overwhelmed by the juxtaposition he presented to her. It was a stark reminder that Inigo Vellanoweth was the complete antithesis of her father in all ways. Inigo was a man who had found a way to bring honour to his money making, whereas her father sought only to benefit himself and anyone who stood in his way be damned.

'You are so very clean, Inigo,' she said at last, soft envy in her tone. 'I am not like you. I am so very dirty. I've been surrounded by corruption for years.' He'd been surrounded by those who'd nurtured a strong sense of duty and civic pride while she'd been boxed in on all sides by men who worshipped only money. 'And I'm selfish. You seek to help others, but, by running away, I am only helping myself.' The old guilt was back. Perhaps the things she wanted to run away from couldn't be outrun. 'Like father like daughter. Perhaps I can't change that.' It was one of her greatest fears, that after all this it simply wouldn't matter.

Inigo shook his head. 'You *are* good and brave and kind, Audevere. You are not defined by your father. Leaving proves that. The way you treated your maid, the way you worried over her, the way you worried over Collin. You have a heart, a good heart, Aud. You left to protect Tremblay, to protect unknown others that might have come after him. You gave up a life of ease and luxury. Those are selfless acts.'

That's because you don't know, her mind whispered. She wasn't only tainted by association, nor was it tied to her father's dirty dealings. She'd been tainted since birth.

Chapter Seventeen

They reached Exeter an hour before dusk on market day. The innyard was bustling as Inigo went in to check on their room. Tomorrow they would arrive at Merry Weather, seat of the Boscastle Dukes, by afternoon. Their sojourn on the road would be over and Inigo couldn't help but wonder what else might be over with it.

They would have to stop pretending to be man and wife. They would have to stop pretending the road could go on for ever, that they didn't have to deal with the threat posed by her father. Inigo wondered if her disclosure today in the carriage had been an attempt to start establishing distance between them. Perhaps she'd expected him to be put off by a glimpse into her life with her father and how she'd been used. If that had been the case, it had most definitely failed. If there'd ever been anyone in need of protection, it was Audevere Brenley. She'd been robbed of so much, treated so vilely, that it broke his heart. It made his blood pound and his temper flare. He wanted to challenge every man who'd wronged her until there was no one left to hurt her, including her own father. He wanted to gather her to him and keep her safe until she *believed* she was safe. Was she any closer to believing that at the end of their journey than she had been at the beginning?

The innkeeper came back with a key and Inigo left instructions for their luggage to be taken up. He wasn't quite ready to retire yet. He wanted one more walk with his 'wife'.

At the carriage, Inigo helped her down, taking care to avoid the dirtier parts of the yard. 'Shall we walk through the market before it closes?' Inigo suggested. 'I thought we could put together a dinner of our own, unless you fancy eating in the taproom? There's no question of obtaining a private parlour tonight, we're too late to bespeak.' He felt himself smile as he said the words, though, recalling the reason they were too late.

'A picnic dinner in our room sounds perfect.' Audevere smiled, perhaps her own thoughts running along similar lines as his—that this was their last night before everything changed, before real life returned.

They made smart bargains at the market, bartering for deals with the merchants who were eager to sell the last of their goods, close up shop and go home for the evening. They filled their basket with a bottle of wine, a loaf of bread, a wheel of cheese, pears, half a chicken still warm from the spit and the last of the baker's blackberry tarts.

'It might be more food than we can eat!' Audevere exclaimed with a laugh, but both of them were loath to leave the market. To eat their last supper together was one step closer to an ending they didn't want to discuss. They lingered over the craft booths. He caught Audevere admiring a necklace—a polished aventurine pendant that hung on a thin silver chain.

'You should have it,' Inigo whispered at her ear. 'Will you allow me to buy my wife a gift?'

Audevere turned with a shake of her head, her own voice low. 'I am not really your wife.'

He kissed her then, not caring who saw. 'Tonight you are.' He gestured to the silversmith. 'We'll take the necklace. Wrap it up for me; it matches my wife's eyes.' Then he took her hand and pulled her to another booth.

'Inigo! What are you doing?' she scolded with a laugh that said whatever he was doing she didn't mind too much.

'I am in the mood to give gifts, dear wife.' He gave her a teasing smile as he called the man at the booth over. 'My wife needs a little knife, something sharp and wicked she can carry with her when she goes out,' Inigo told the man.

'If my wife was that pretty, I'd never let her go out alone. Let me see what I have.' He came back with a collection of flat, slim boxes and took the lids off each one. 'A *sgian dubh* would serve your wife well. It's small and sharp.'

* * *

Oh, sweet heavens, Inigo meant to buy her a knife! Because of her story today. Her throat thickened and tears welled up. She'd barely kept from crying when he'd bought her the necklace. But what this meant was beyond words. Inigo hefted one of the blades, testing it for balance, and handed it to her. 'Try this one.' It had a claddagh symbol done in pewter on the hilt and the blade gleamed. It was a pretty but lethal weapon.

She took it tentatively. What did one look for? What was she supposed to notice? She felt clumsy and a little foolish. She handed it back to Inigo. 'You choose for me.'

'This one, then.' His eyes lingered on hers in a way that made her wish they were already back in their room. 'No one will ever touch you again against your will, Audevere,' he murmured, making her blood heat with desire. All she wanted was for him to touch her, for him to be the only man who ever touched her again. 'This blade is my promise. You will never be helpless again.'

It was a generous gift, a kind gift, but the words brought home the reality of what they faced. Was he preparing them for goodbye with those words? *When I'm not there to protect you myself.* She did not want to think about that time to come and yet she must. Her last secret still sat between them and, once it was revealed, he would see it, too: there was no future for them.

She slipped the *sgian dubh* into her skirt pocket. The weight of it was reassuring, just like the feel of Inigo's arm beneath her hand as they made their way back to the inn. Steel and muscle and hers for one night more.

They reached the top of the stairs and Inigo unlocked the door, ushering her inside. The room was clean but tiny. A small fire had already been lit to warm the room. 'Penny for your thoughts, Aud? Or are they worth more than that?' Inigo set the basket on the small table by the window. 'You've been quiet since we left the market.'

'I'm not ready for this to end. I'm not ready for real life, for my father's threats. None of it.' Audevere sank down on the dark-blue-and-white counterpane. She had difficult decisions to make in the days ahead. Secretly, in her heart, she didn't want there to be a time when Inigo wasn't there to protect her. But that time couldn't exist, *didn't* exist. Disappearing meant letting go of this incredible man. It could not be otherwise.

'We don't have to be ready just yet.' Inigo came to her. He knelt before her, working off her half-boots and setting them aside. He stripped off her stockings, taking her feet in his hands and rubbing them. 'Are you hungry? Can dinner wait?' His cool blue eyes fired, sending a shaft of hot awareness through her.

She gave him a coy smile in answer. 'It depends on what dinner is waiting for.'

'Me.' Inigo rose up and bore her backwards to the

bed, taking her mouth with his, finding the place at her neck where her pulse beat. He kissed it and she felt it flutter. Yes, this, a thousand times this, her heart cried out. This and only this could keep away the inevitable. He undressed her as he went, his hands working open the frogs of her jacket, the buttons of her linen blouse beneath, pushing the silk chemise up and over her breasts until they were bare for his mouth, for his tongue, for his teeth. He licked her, sucked her until she cried out from the heat he built inside her, from the warm damp that he caused to pool between her legs and the thrum that hummed at her core. But he did not relent.

He was on his knees before her, pushing up her skirts in great bunching fistfuls until his mouth could find her, claim her. His tongue ran a tickling, torturing line up her seam to the hidden nub of her, working her to a frenzy until she begged him to complete it, to push her over the edge.

'Not without me, not tonight,' Inigo panted, his own breathing shallow from exertion as he rose up from her thighs, covering her, reaching her hands and shackling them as he thrust into her hard. Yes, this was so much better. To explode with him inside her, to have him with her in that final moment. Her hips arched into his, the pace they set, frenetic, as if they could not explode fast enough, hard enough. But even pushed to their limits, his first thoughts were of her. While she screamed her release, his own body taut beneath her fingertips as he reached his achievement, he spent himself into the sheets before they both lay back exhausted.

She wanted to be exhausted for ever. She couldn't think, couldn't form words, couldn't even form thoughts. She was aware of Inigo drawing a blanket up over them, of nestling against his shoulder, both of them in varying stages of undress.

Then she was aware of little else until the room was full dark and a candle flickered on the little table by the window, a table that had been transformed with plates and silverware, their findings from the market laid out on a platter. The common meal had been transformed. As had the man who'd prepared it.

Inigo turned from the window with a smile. 'You're awake. When I said dinner could wait, I had no idea it might be a couple of hours.' He'd washed and changed, discarding his travelling clothes for his blue banyan. It belted at the waist, but where it gaped, she could see he was wearing nothing beneath it. 'I've laid your things out and there's warm water for washing,' he offered. 'Change into something more comfortable and I'll pour the wine.'

It might have been the most decadent meal she would ever eat, Audevere thought as she took her seat, dressed in her nightgown with her hair down. Across from her, Inigo looked darkly handsome and entirely wicked as he served her. 'You're far more romantic than I ever thought.' She wanted to remember him like this, his passionate nature on full display. 'It's always the quiet ones who have the wildest sides.'

He met her comment evenly. 'And it's always the boldest who have the most to hide. You're far less of an open book than you pretend.' He handed her a wineglass. 'Here's to discoveries. Here's to wild sides and hidden sides.'

'Here's to making them last,' Audevere answered as their glasses clinked. There were other things she would say if she were braver, other stories she would tell him, other words she must utter. But she could not bring herself to do it. They were both desperate tonight, desperate to make the night last, to put off tomorrow, to hold on to the wonderful things they had discovered amid the difficulties they faced. She recognised his desperation in the gifts he'd bought her. They were not the sort of presents a man could give a woman who was not his intended or his wife. But he wanted her to have something to remember him by; the gifts, even the lovemaking, had carried the message of goodbye. She wondered if this was how honeymooning couples felt when a return was imminent. But while they had their whole lives to look forward to, Inigo and Audevere had only hours.

She sipped her wine. 'Tell me about your family, Inigo.' She might as well start preparing. Forewarned was forearmed and perhaps it would be easier to do it by candlelight; perhaps the plunge to earth would be softer. 'You mentioned you had sisters? A little brother? For the longest time, I thought you were an only child.'

Inigo leaned back in his chair, the candlelight playing over the smooth expanse of the chest she knew so well where his banyan gaped open. 'Well, I was an only child for several years—fourteen of them, to be exact.' His smile faded and sadness touched his eyes. 'There was a long gap between me and my sisters. You should know, since you'll no doubt see the crosses in the Merry Weather cemetery, that after me there were two brothers and a sister who didn't live past infancy.'

'Do you remember them being born?' Audevere asked softly. She couldn't imagine such tragedy touching the Vellanoweths. They seemed above it somehow.

'Two of them. The first was born when I was barely two. Then I was five and eight. I held them, with my father's help, of course.' He made a cradle with his arms and her heart constricted a little at the thought of Inigo with a child. 'I was excited to have a brother and a sister,' he told her. 'Eaton and Cassian had sisters and a little brother each. It seemed like that was how it was supposed to be, but not for us.' He remembered when they'd died, too. But she didn't ask. She didn't have to. She saw it in his eyes. How sad for him growing up. But he wouldn't let her pity him.

'Vennor was an only child, too. I didn't feel alone. I had Cassian and Eaton and Vennor, and for many years they were the only brothers I had. In many ways they still are. My brother, Benny, is only ten years old,' he told Audevere. 'A late-life surprise, my mother likes to say. It was a worrisome pregnancy, though, so unexpected at her age.'

'How old are your sisters?' Audevere reached for the blackberry tarts and served them.

'Sarah is sixteen and Mary Rose is fourteen. They *dream* of London, incessantly.' He smiled as he spoke of his sisters. 'I was grown when they were born, off at school and later in London so I am more like a young uncle to all of them.' But he loved them all, that much was plain. No wonder he was such a natural protector. That role had been shaped for him in his early years, loving and losing the infant siblings, then being so much older than the siblings that had finally come.

She poured the last of the wine. 'Your family sounds very loving, very wonderful.' And very different from hers.

'My family will love you. My sisters will adore you, they'll want to know all the fashions from London, and Ben loves everyone, so you needn't worry on that account.'

'Who says I was worried?' Audevere replied drily.

'You didn't have to say anything.' Inigo rose from the table and offered her his hand. 'Do you think we might take a break from discussing my family?'

'What did you have in mind?' Audevere took his hand and let him draw her against him.

'Dessert in bed. Starting with drinking the rest of my wine from your navel and licking my blackberry tart from your breasts,' he growled against her ear, his teeth finding her lobe.

'That sounds positively delicious.'

Chapter Eighteen

They dressed slowly in the morning, the usual rituals taking on a certain reverence as if they were arming one another for battle like squires of old. She tied his cravat with exacting precision. She held up her hair, giving him access to the slim length of her neck as he fastened the necklace from the market. She felt his hands linger as he breathed her in. There was comfort in knowing he was savouring these moments, too, filing them away for a rainy day. She turned towards him, her fingers touching the stone where it lay against her skin. 'How does it look?'

Inigo leaned against the bedpost, taking her in with hot eyes that said he wished they were back in bed. 'Beautiful. How could it not when it's worn by you? You make everything lovely, Audevere.' She stored the compliment deep in her heart right next to the others. Some day she would be able to take them all out and remember these moments: the last time they'd leave an inn together, the last breakfast, the last carriage ride, the last leg of the journey.

Audevere made a point of cataloguing each in her mind, a picture collection of what these days had meant to her. She'd not wanted to need a man when this had begun, not after her experiences which had proven a woman was better off alone, but now she needed Inigo as much as she wanted her freedom. Or perhaps *more* than she wanted her freedom. But it was too late in the game to change her position and there was still the final ugly truth which would drive him away for good. She had to claim her freedom, it was all she could do.

They took the final bend and Merry Weather came into view down a long drive, all pale-brown brick and elegance, two wings emanating from either side of a wide, columned brick square. 'That centre section was built first, by the original Duke of Boscastle in the sixteenth century,' Inigo explained, seeing her interest. 'The others added on in their time.'

It was imposing. This was the sort of old wealth her father envied and could never acquire. Its simple, powerful lines put his gaudy town house with all its affectations to shame. The carriage passed through a gate, two pillars on either side marking the official entrance to Merry Weather, and a new wave of panic took Audevere. 'Do they know we're coming?' The only thing worse that having to receive the daughter of one's nemesis was to have her arrive by surprise.

'I sent word ahead when we started planning this effort of yours. They know we're coming and they know why. I've told them everything. You needn't be embarrassed about your past.' Inigo was all calm assurance and she wished she could borrow some of that confidence for herself. Even after his encouragement last night, she still couldn't quite believe she'd be accepted. Maybe acceptance was too much to hope for. Perhaps she would be tolerated and that would have to be enough. After all, she didn't need anything more from them. She would be gone, she reminded herself. What the Vellanoweths thought of her ultimately didn't matter. Yet she would be lying to herself if she said she believed that. She fingered the necklace, rubbing the smooth stone absently in her hand for comfort.

Inigo's hand reached out and covered hers, bringing it down to her lap, his gaze steady. 'They will love you.'

'They just have to tolerate me,' she voiced the words out loud.

Inigo laughed. 'They will do more than tolerate you.' Because he asked it of them, Audevere thought. How wondrous to be surrounded by such people, to be able to call upon them in a time of need.

As the carriage drew closer, figures appeared on the steps, women in starched aprons and pressed grey dresses, men in blue livery, and at the top of the steps arrayed from youngest to oldest, stood the Duke of Boscastle and his family. Something in her throat caught as she glanced at Inigo. On the road, just the two of them, it was easy to forget who he was in real life, or what it meant to be a duke's heir. They'd turned out for him, of course. It was what servants did when the heir returned.

The carriage halted and Audevere swallowed hard, fighting the sensation that this was what it would be like to be Mrs Vellanoweth in truth. Only she wouldn't ever be Mrs Vellanoweth, even in a perfect world. Inigo's wife would be Lady Tintagel and eventually the Duchess of Boscastle. More than that, though, when the carriage door opened, she felt she had come home. And she could not afford to feel that way about a place she would leave in a short while.

Inigo stepped out first and offered her his hand. 'Smile, my dear, there is nothing to fear here.' Her hand slid into his and he squeezed it. 'They *will* love you,' he whispered, 'as do I.' The last was said so softly she wondered if she had imagined it. Perhaps it was only her wishing that made the words feel like they had been said. Perhaps it was just the echo of the words etched on her heart.

Inigo's father stepped forward, a tall, elegant, older version of his son. 'Welcome to Merry Weather, Miss Brenley. I hope you will enjoy your time with us.'

They did love her, as much as she would let them. The love and care of strangers was new and uncharted territory for her. She'd been loved by her mother, had never doubted that love. But they'd lived reclusively, nothing like this where she was surrounded by people all day. Inigo's sisters were as delightful as he'd promised, eager to try out new hairstyles and talk of fashion. His little brother was endlessly energetic and their days were filled with long, laughing walks up on the windy bluffs where Merry Weather overlooked the sea. There were hearty suppers, which the whole family, Benny included, ate together, laughing and talking, sometimes arguing. His sisters were well educated and held informed opinions about politics and the economy. Afterwards, there was always entertainment in the family parlour; she and Inigo taught the girls whist or she watched Inigo play chess with his father, a pastime that clearly delighted them both. It made her smile to see them together, father and son. This was what it meant to be a family. It was a beautiful and rare thing. No wonder the Cornish Dukes protected their own with such tenacity. Who would not? This was a great treasure indeed.

'You needn't be afraid, my dear.' The Duchess took a chair next to her in the family parlour and took out her needlework. Tonight the girls were taking turns at the piano while Inigo played draughts with Benny while their father looked on offering snippets of advice. 'We won't vanish, nor will we break. You keep looking at us as if we are delicate china.' She smiled fondly. 'We are not. We have weathered our share of disappointments and are all the stronger for it.' She nodded towards Inigo. 'He is a good brother to his siblings even though he's so much older. For a while we thought he might be the only family we'd have.'

'Your family is extraordinary,' Audevere said. 'I've never known anything like it.'

'No one's life is perfect and we can't choose the families we're born into, only the families we make by gathering those we love about us and keeping them safe.'

Gathering. Keeping. Loving. These were not part of Audevere's plan. Running. Forgetting. That was her plan, although these days it seemed even that decision was in question when pitted up against the love and acceptance of the Vellanoweths. She let her gaze drift to the table where Inigo sat with Benny and his father. She needed to be strong. If Inigo thought her decision was in doubt, he'd press all the harder for her to stay. She was going to have to decide soon. Any day now, a letter would arrive from her father, a response to Inigo's threat of exposure. It wouldn't take him long to realise where they'd gone and the game would be in motion once more, this idyllic hiatus over. She wondered if the Vellanoweths would love her then? She told herself she didn't want to be here to find out.

'Have you decided what to do with her? We can give her the cottage in Devonshire if she's amenable,' Inigo's father asked in quiet tones as they strolled the

cliff path above the sea. Audevere was up ahead with
his sisters and Ben, the dogs romping at their heels,
their laughter floating back to him on the wind. It
was uncannily close to the picture he'd formed in his
mind, of seeing her with his family and it pleased
him. Inigo wondered if it pleased his father.

'It's only been a week,' Inigo answered, his gaze
never leaving the moving tableau ahead of them. He
liked watching Audevere with the girls. The three-
some was at ease and they'd taken to one another almost instantly. The girls had embraced her warmly,
eager to make friends, and Audevere had responded
with all the warmth Inigo knew was in her, genuinely
appreciative of their welcome. They consulted with
her on everything from necklaces to hairdos. He'd
found them just yesterday in the conservatory, sitting beside the fountain braiding one another's hair
and trying new styles. 'She remains intractable on
the cottage.' Audevere's stubbornness was proving
frustrating. Why did she resist? Surely now she understood they would be able to overcome her father.

'Brenley's response should arrive any day. We
have to be ready with a plan.' A lack of a response
would indicate Brenley was calling his bluff, forcing him to send the letter to the King as he had
threatened. But neither he nor his father believed
that would be the direction Brenley would take. It
would ruin Brenley. Beside him, his father halted,
gathering his thoughts carefully before he spoke.

Inigo gave his father time to frame his opinion.

His family had not disappointed him. From the moment he'd arrived at Merry Weather with Audevere, his family had welcomed them, surrounding them with all the famous Boscastle hospitality. His mother had seen to it that Audevere had gowns aplenty and a maid. His father had been unfailingly kind to her, treating her as if she were an honoured guest instead of Sir Gismond Brenley's daughter. Yet, Inigo knew his father worried about his decision to bring her here and his plan for how to handle Brenley.

'Brenley will not tolerate your threat to expose him. You have cornered him and that makes him dangerous. He knows you can ruin him for decent society and take his title. He will strike back hard.' His father paused. 'I fear he may ask for a duel. That is a very permanent way to settle the feud between you and him. Although, once his temper cools, he might realise that if he killed you, there would be six others waiting to face him. He cannot hope to win against all of us.' His father shook his head. 'Of course, to lose you would be devastating. The damage to us would already be done. Even if one of us shot him, it wouldn't bring you back. I would not want him to issue the challenge.'

'I would win,' Inigo assured him seriously, 'and all our problems would be solved. He could not threaten us or the people of Cornwall again with his selfish schemes.'

His father put a hand on his shoulder. 'Son, it will not bring Collin back. I know you swore an oath when Collin died to avenge his death. But I do not think either he or Richard would want vengeance and honour pursued at the end of a pistol.'

'It may be the only option.' Inigo's response was terse. Inigo felt his father's quiet frustration, although, to his credit, his father did not argue with him.

'Have you discussed that possibility with Audevere?' They continued walking, his father's gaze studying him.

'No.' There was no lying to his father. There never had been. His father demanded honesty from his children in all things, even now as adults. Inigo remembered learning that lesson the hard way growing up, but he'd only had to learn it once.

'How do you think she'd feel if you fought a duel with her father, knowing that only one of you is likely to come away from it alive?'

Inigo had no answer for that. 'She wants to be free of him. He has used her sorely in the past, in ways that are reprehensible to consider. No parent should use a child the way she was used.'

His father nodded. 'Even a bad parent is still a parent, though, and, from what I understand, he is all she has in this world.' There was a question underlying his words.

'She has us,' Inigo answered the question as implicitly as it was asked.

'Does she? Is that what you intend, then?' They'd reached the end of the headlands and they stood looking out over the grey rollers tipped in white. The others were a little way off, trying to fly Ben's kite and having little success, but loads of fun. 'You mean to make her one of us? You mean to marry Audevere Brenley?'

'I mean to offer her more than a cottage in Devonshire.' Inigo had not put it to himself so bluntly before. He'd always allowed the idea to remain rather amorphous in his mind. 'Yes, I do,' Inigo answered, feeling the reality of that settle on his shoulders, part-elation, part-trepidation. What if she wouldn't have him? What if his parents disagreed with his choice? What if the Cornish Dukes disapproved? 'How would you and Mother feel if I made her my wife?' Inigo tested the hypothesis. His family was important to him. He would not cause a rift if it could be avoided.

'I think it would depend on the reasons.' His father slanted him a look. 'If you love her and she loves you, it is one thing. But if you are marrying her to protect her, that's another. I would have misgivings in that regard. If this marriage is for any other reason than love, we will find another way to protect her.'

A smile played on his father's face as they looked out over the water. 'Do you know how many times I've imagined having this talk with you? Ever since the day you were born, I think I began rehearsing for all the milestones in your life. The first day you went off to boarding school, the first day you came up to town as a young man, the first day you took your own rooms in London and the day you decided to marry.' His father's blue eyes were misty as he shook his head. 'But never, in all my imaginings of that moment, did I think the woman you might choose would be the daughter of *our* rival. I want you to be careful, Son.

'You know how your mother and I feel about marriage, Inigo. It should be for no other reason than love because marriage is for ever and it is meant to be lived together.' His father arched his dark brows. 'So, you both need to ask yourselves whether you love one another enough to bear the hardships of life. Your mother and I have buried three children, we've buried our friends, we've buried our friends' children. The two of you would start married life under a cloud if you duel with her father.'

With blood on his hands, Inigo thought more baldly. 'I love her. I've loved her for quite a while, even before I knew her as I know her now,' Inigo confessed. It felt good, cleansing, to say the words out loud. He'd not realised how much he'd bottled up inside, how much he'd kept from himself and from others.

His father chuckled. 'Does she know what you intend?'

'Perhaps she might have guessed, but likely not the reason for it.' Inigo grinned at his father. 'I suppose I should put that on my list of things I must discuss with her.' He would find a way to make Audevere stay, to convince her that marriage was possible, that their love was possible. It didn't have to end with the journey.

'The sooner the better.' His father put a hand on his shoulder. 'I wish you luck, because I see what she means to you. But remember, Audevere Brenley has been through a lot. She may not be able to give you what you want. If she wants to fly, you should not hold her back. No happiness can come from that.'

Inigo turned to watch her with the others, the wind catching at her hat. She looked happy and the colour in her cheeks was high. Perhaps she wouldn't want to leave. Perhaps she loved his family and Merry Weather as much as he did, or at least enough to stay. He'd done his best to woo her with all the temptations a family could offer. But his father was right. It was time to have those difficult conversations and it was best to do it now while there was at least the illusion of free will before Gismond Brenley showed his hand. If he and Audevere could decide what it was they wanted without any interference, it would give them a foundation for going forward. 'I will discuss it with her tonight. As for Brenley, I think it's time to call the Dukes and assemble our council of war.'

She waved to him, a smile on her face, one hand on her hat to keep it from flying away. He waved back and strode towards her, joining in the fun of kite flying in the sea wind. He wasn't above sweetening the pot—anything he could do to hedge his bets, to convince her they could make a life here.

Chapter Nineteen

The impossible had happened. Inigo had become a chatterbox. It was Audevere's first indication that something was on his mind. The second was the break in routine. Instead of joining the family after dinner, Inigo suggested a walk in the gallery. It was beginning to worry her and she could think of only one reason for it. 'Has there been word from my father?' In truth, the waiting weighed on her. She was not long on patience. It was hard waiting for the other shoe to fall, knowing that it would, but not what it would be. What action would her father take? What action would Inigo be required to take in response? Her own decisions would be contingent on both of theirs. She'd rather make those decisions before she had any more emotion attached to them. It would be too easy to stay at Merry Weather, to let Inigo handle the mess that was her father. But that would all change once Inigo knew her secret.

Inigo shook his head. 'No, there's been no word.'

Audevere smiled. 'Then what's on your mind?'

'Can't I just want to be alone with you?' He pulled her to him and stole a kiss. There'd been precious little time for kisses, stolen or otherwise, this week. She'd missed them.

'You can, but I don't think that's it.'

Inigo led her over to a wide, square, upholstered bench set in the middle of the gallery and pulled her down beside him. 'You're right. It's something more, something I hope you will take seriously.' His eyes glittered intently in the dim light of the gallery.

'I will, whatever it is,' she promised solemnly, her senses on full alert. Whatever he was thinking about, it was deeply important to him.

'I am asking you to do me the honour of being my wife. I want to marry you, Aud. I want to make a life with you here at Merry Weather, raise our children the way I was raised, amid a loving family and friends.'

She was silent, stunned. It was a simple but perfect proposal, all his talk of family and children an apropos match for the setting of the Boscastle gallery where generations of Vellanoweths looked down on them. How long had he been planning such a proposal, to have thought so perfectly about where to ask? But that was Inigo, everything managed down to the last detail.

What to say? Of all the things she'd imagined he'd ask, this was not one of them. Oh, she might have fantasised on the road about being his wife in truth, but she'd never dared to let herself dream of actually being asked. And she dared not dream it now or else she'd give in to it. She had to hold fast to her resolve, she had to remember all the reasons she needed to refuse. 'Now? With so much unsettled? Do you think a proposal is wise?' She opted to prevaricate instead of reject.

'I want this to be about us, Aud. This should be *our* decision.' His hand rubbed soothing circles across her knuckles. 'I love you, Aud. This is not about protection or convenience or a vendetta against your father. This is about you and me. But I worry you might not see that if we wait to hear from your father.'

He loved her. She had not imagined the whispered words after all. She let her heart sing for a moment. The silence stretched between them, one heartbeat, two, and then three. He was waiting for her to say something, to say yes, to say that she loved him, too. She did love him, too much to accept his proposal. She knew what she had to do, what she had to tell him.

'I am honoured by your proposal, truly,' Audevere said, clearing her throat against the thickness lodged there. He was forever reducing her to the point of tears. There'd been so much goodness in her life these past weeks with him and now she had to throw it away in order to save him. 'But there's something you don't know and it will change your mind. I won't hold you to your proposal.' She held his eyes, preparing him for the blow as she reached into her pocket and pulled out two miniatures. 'These are my mothers. Both of them. I am Gismond Brenley's natural daughter.'

She waited for him to digest that, to translate it into its cruder term: bastard. A child born outside the benefit of wedlock. 'My mother, the woman who gave birth to me, was a French actress. My father had a woman in every port. She died in childbirth and my father brought me home to his legal, childless wife.' She gave a brittle laugh. 'Some wives hope their husbands bring home silks and spices from their voyages. Hers brought home a squalling infant, two weeks old.' It would have been easy for her mother to be furious, to scorn the baby. But her mother had embraced her as her own daughter. 'All I have of my birth mother is my looks and my name. She called me Audevere for the French Queen. I have a small miniature of her. I am unmistakably hers.'

'Oh, my dear girl, I am so sorry.' Inigo handed the miniatures back to her, but he did not walk away.

'I'm not,' Audevere was quick to answer. 'The woman I know as my mother loved me. I would not have missed her love for the world. My father could have left me at an orphanage, on a church step. He had one noble moment and it was likely the saving of me. My mother never begrudged me my origins.'

'And neither do I.' Inigo stared at the miniatures in her hand. The likeness between Audevere and her birth mother was unmistakable—both blonde, green-eyed beauties with eyes that sparked with a passion for living. So this was the secret she'd harboured in fear all these years, the Sword of Damocles her father had held over her head in order to ensure she did his bidding.

'But you must,' Audevere explained. 'If you marry me, my father will hold the secret of my birth over you in order to ensure your compliance in all things.' She was insistent. 'A nobleman cannot take a bastard to wife. You know that as well as I. He would be laughed at, reviled by his peers. He would do anything to prevent that from happening, even participate in my father's schemes. And he'd be well rewarded.'

Inigo nodded, understanding the complexity of what she'd revealed. 'This is why you opposed the match with Tremblay.' But it was more than that. In a wave of shocking clarity, he saw the antecedents of that decision. 'This is why you broke with Collin, to save him.'

Audevere rose from the bench and Inigo let her go, giving her the space to pace, and she spoke, her hands tight at her waist. 'It was my father's idea to threaten to break it off with Collin in order to get him to comply with my father's wishes to build that road of his in Porth Karrek. My father was disappointed and somewhat surprised by the amount of resistance Collin put up about the road once he understood how many people would be displaced from their homes and forced to relocate under their own power. It would cost people jobs and money they didn't have. Collin felt it was wrong, but my father didn't care and wouldn't listen to his arguments.'

Inigo nodded. He remembered how upset Collin had been over the road and how ashamed he'd been over his own naivety to invest in the scheme without fully understanding the circumstances until it was too late. He'd been proud of his friend for standing up to Brenley even at that late date. But it had not changed Brenley's mind; it had only forced Brenley to up the stakes and he'd done so with the threat of losing Audevere.

'When I refused to end my engagement, my father revealed the truth about my parentage. That's when I agreed to break it off with Collin, because I could see it was in his best interest to let me go. I liked Collin, perhaps I even thought I loved him. I didn't want to let him go. But I needed to for his own good. So I did what my father asked, not for my father's sake, or for mine, but for Collin's.' The grief on her face touched Inigo at his core. All those years when he'd been blaming her, she'd been suffering, too. She'd told him as much earlier, that evening at the Bradfords', but to hear the detailed account was heart-rending. She had suffered her grief alone whereas his grief had been shared among friends. 'I didn't save him, though, did I? I killed him instead.'

'No, Aud. He made his choice.' Inigo went to her and wrapped her in his arms. The words were for

them both. There was nothing either of them could
have done, he saw that now as he listened to Audevere's tale. 'For years, I thought there must have been
something I could have done. But when I hear your
tale, and see your guilt, I realise that's not true.' This
whole journey had been moving towards forgiving
themselves for Collin.

'He took his own life and, in doing so, he might
have saved mine,' Audevere whispered, her face
pressed to his shoulder. 'If Collin hadn't stood up to
my father, I wouldn't have been forced to look more
closely at my father's business dealings, to question
how he'd achieved his wealth. I began to see the tac-
tics he used and I began to see my part it in. I had
been an unwitting accomplice, another pawn for him
to move around his chessboard. I saw, too, how my
luxuries had been acquired at the expense of others.'

She paused and tipped her face up to him. 'I rode
over to Porth Karrek one day. I saw the people who'd
been displaced by the road my father wanted to build.
I suppose I didn't want to believe it. I wanted Collin to be wrong. But he wasn't. Inigo, they were the
poorest people I'd ever seen. They were ragged and
dirty, living in lean-tos along the side of the road,
begging for food, for work. They had nowhere to go.
My father had demolished their houses and not com-
pensated them for it. Why should he? They had no
voice, no vote. What could they do to him?'

He tried to offer comfort. 'Collin tried to compen-
sate them, tried to relocate some of them to Hayle

on his father's land, but he couldn't save them all.'
Inigo remembered the little girl who had died in Collin's arms as they'd ridden towards his father's estate. She'd been small and hungry and the slightest
chill had carried her off. Collin had wept over her
for days, right before he'd set off on his fatal swim.

He smoothed back her hair and framed her face
with his hands. 'I understand why you told me all
that and I understand why you fear marrying, Aud.
But your father can't get to me. Your father could
never leverage you against me, not your loyalty or
your birth. Anything he did would trigger that letter being sent to the King. He would be ruined. You
are free to make your own decision.'

'You are relentless.' Audevere gave him a faint
smile. 'I think we should both revisit this in a couple
of days when emotions have settled and we're both
thinking clearly.' Then she wrapped her arms about
his waist and held him tight. 'I've missed you in my
bed, Inigo Vellanoweth.'

Inigo kissed the top of her head. 'And I've missed
you in mine.' She had not accepted his offer, but at
least she had not refused him outright. A few days
ago, she would have put up a fight. He smiled to
himself. The race was not always to the fast. He was
making steady progress. And just in time.

The letter arrived the next day. It was good timing as far as Inigo was concerned. Inigo wanted to
get this over with, wanted to get on with his life now

that he knew what it was he wanted above all else: a life with Audevere, a life here at Merry Weather with his family. He would have liked to have spent today celebrating his engagement when his friends arrived, but that celebration would have to wait. Audevere had made it plain she would decide nothing until the situation with her father was settled. But none of those things was within his power to ensure. He had to settle instead for what he could celebrate. She had not said no and she had trusted him with the darkest secret of her heart.

'Should I have waited?' his father asked as he settled across from him at the desk, the letter already open in front of him.

'No. Best to get it over with and move on to happier times.' Inigo scanned it, then read it once more, slowly, a cold smile playing on his lips. 'Brenley wants me to make an honest woman of his daughter in reparation for having run off with her. He's in Truro awaiting our response.' He passed the letter to his father. 'It seems for once we are in agreement on something.' How could he and Brenley suddenly be on the same side? Something wasn't right.

His father reached for his reading glasses. 'Why does Brenley think he's in any position to make demands? You're the one with the letter to the King. I should think that trumps anything Brenley can do.'

'Brenley is betting that I will protect her, that I will do what it takes to keep her secret safe. If I marry her, he won't tell the world she's his natural daughter. And if I do marry her, how can I possibly go to the King and defame my father-in-law without dragging us all into scandal?' Brenley meant to use Audevere as a double-edged sword. Marry her to protect her, marry her and in Brenley's mind she became eternal leverage against him. There was no escaping him.

He was glad he'd spoken to her of marriage last night in advance of her father's letter. He didn't want her to doubt the source of his offer. His offer came from his heart, not from any sense of obligation, coerced there by her father's threats.

'I applaud your sentiment, but let's be honest about what marriage accomplishes.' His father looked over the rims of his glasses. 'Gismond Brenley will be a thorn in your side for ever if you do this. You will never be rid of him. Son, marriage won't protect either of you. The only person it protects in Gismond Brenley.' Otherwise the man wouldn't have suggested the alliance. Inigo saw that now. They'd played right into his hands. They might as well have never left London. How could he marry Audevere now without appearing to capitulate to Brenley? A marriage would allow Brenley to save face. Perhaps Brenley had known that and had liked putting the Sisyphean dilemma to him.

'Perhaps it's time to walk away,' his father offered, prompting an examination of options.

Inigo's temper blazed at the suggestion. 'From

her? From the vow I made Collin? From all the people who will be Brenley's victims in the future?'

His father sat back in his chair, hands laced over his flat stomach. 'How do you propose to stop him?'

They had long played at this exercise when his father had taught him about estate management. His father would propose a problem and Inigo would offer solutions. But back then, it had all been hypothetical.

'I will send the letter to the King and expose him for everything he's done and we will ride out the storm.'

He'd show the King what the displaced poor had suffered for the Porth Karrek road that ran ore to the big city factories, the faulty munitions facility whose ammunition Brenley had transported to British troops during the Peninsular Wars. He'd been lauded a hero for his daring run, but one in five bullets had misfired. Soldiers had died counting on those bullets while he'd been awarded his knighthood.

'He will be angry. He will strike back before he's down and out entirely,' his father warned. 'There will be consequences for such an action.'

'Then let him challenge me. A duel would settle everything once and for all. I'll send the note and have Eaton act as my second when he arrives.'

Chapter Twenty

A duel! Audevere backed away from the door and staggered into an alcove. She sat down hard on the little bench set in the niche, grateful for the privacy the spot afforded her. The letter had come. She'd suspected as much when Inigo's father had summoned him to the office. Duelling was not her father's way. Her father preferred threats and blackmail, covert actions that occurred behind the scenes in the murky grey area of the law.

She pressed a hand to her stomach. One of them would die, Inigo or her father, and it would be on her head. She'd set up her father to kill the man she loved and she'd set the man she loved up to kill her father. Her conscience was laughing hard at her. This was a dilemma worthy of a Shakespeare play and all because she'd wanted to be free. Now she would have neither her freedom nor the man she loved.

She put a hand to her mouth to hold back the tears. What had she thought to accomplish by bringing Inigo into all this? Why hadn't she found a way to do this on her own? Perhaps she should have just walked out the door with the clothes on her back one day and taken her chances. If she had done that, none of this would have happened.

None of it, whispered her heart. Not the journey by coach with Inigo all to herself for days on end, not those beautiful nights when he'd made love to her at the inn, not the days at Merry Weather, full of autumn picnics, kite flying and romping on the cliffs with his family, not the chance to purge her guilt to the person to whom it mattered most. To have the chance to love Inigo Vellanoweth even if only for a short time. Would she really want to have missed all that?

She drew a deep breath to steady herself. She'd known it would come to this. There was no purpose in second-guessing herself now. If she really loved him, she'd leave him. He could not be compelled to marry someone who wasn't there to be married. But that wouldn't stop the duel. To do that, she had to get to her father first, to try to talk him out of it, to bargain with him. Her father was at the town house in Truro. She would slip away at dawn.

'There you are!' Mary Rose startled her. 'We've been looking all over for you. Sarah and I want to practise the Dutch braids you were showing us.'

Audevere gave a small smile and took the girl's hand. There was no time like the present to start saying her goodbyes. 'Let's stop by my room first. There's some pink ribbon we can use.'

She made little gifts in her own way the rest of the afternoon; the pink ribbon delighted the girls and she spent time doing puzzles on the library floor with Benny when the rain foiled his plans for an afternoon of kite flying. The gift of time was the best thing she could think of to give the ten-year-old boy. Besides, it was all she had. She remembered how much her mother's time had meant to her, all those afternoons spent dressing her doll or stitching clothes for it. She played the piano after dinner because the Duchess asked her to and blushed when she complimented her, knowing full well she played aptly but simply.

'Well, it's perfect for an evening at home,' the Duchess assured her as she sat back down to play some more. The girls were doing needlepoint, Benjamin was building with blocks while Inigo and his father read political essays. It was a domestic family scene and the perfection of it put a lump in her throat as she played. She wanted to remember this always. Most of all, she wanted to remember the way Inigo looked right now, sitting beside his father, his gaze serious as he leaned over to share something from his reading. Despite his seriousness, he was at ease. Whatever he'd needed to settle in his mind was settled. His decisions were made and they gave him peace. She wished her decisions came with that same peace. But they seemed to come only with regret:

regret if she stayed and regret if she left. Some day she hoped she'd get beyond the regrets.

The clock struck ten and the Duchess rose, gathering her children and herding them upstairs, while her husband and Inigo set aside their reading. 'Shall I walk you up or would you prefer to stay a little longer?' Inigo came to help her put down the lid on the piano.

'I can go up.' Audevere straightened the sheet music, conscious that Inigo's father waited for them both, a stickler for propriety. He would be disappointed to know what she had planned for later tonight for his son.

Upstairs, Inigo saw her to her door, his eyes soft on her as he said goodnight. Inside, she made ready for bed, wearing the pale-pink ensemble she'd worn in Exeter, brushed out her hair and dismissed the maid. It would be an hour before the house settled into sleep, an hour before she could give Inigo his farewell gift. She spent the time packing her valise. In went her four dresses, in went her toiletries. She left out her travelling ensemble, the one she'd worn when she'd fled London. She'd wear it to flee once more. She'd take nothing but her own things despite the Vellanoweths' generosity. She would feel like a thief if she did. It was bad enough she was robbing them of their hospitality, betraying Inigo's belief in her, putting them all in danger. But he would live and he would be free of the Brenleys, and that was more important.

Down the hall, the clock struck eleven in soft chimes. It was time. Audevere tiptoed out of her room and down the hall, a small vial secreted in her hand. Inigo's room was unlocked and she slipped inside, surprised to find him still awake, sitting in the wing-backed chair before the fire, barefoot but otherwise fully dressed, his gaze on the door. 'You're still up,' Audevere said uncertainly. She'd not planned on having to make small talk. Beyond him his bed, an enormous four-poster affair, was turned down but untouched. A brandy sat on the small table beside him, also untouched.

Inigo's eyes moved over her, taking in the pink silk, blue flames starting to flicker in their depths. 'I thought you might come.' His voice was already husky.

'Why did you think that?' She tried to sound casual.

'You were watching me tonight as you played the piano.' He gave her a seductive smile that had her weak in the knees. She knelt before him, ready to engage the game in full and because she didn't trust her knees to hold her much longer.

'Your father would disapprove if he knew I was here,' she whispered, running her hands up the inside of his trousered thighs, spreading his legs, his eyes following her every move.

'He knows I mean to marry you. There would be little harm in anticipating our wedding night at this point.' Inigo's eyes were like blue diamonds, sharp and piercing, as they challenged her. Perhaps this was one challenge she would not rise to. He was hoping she was here in reconsideration of her answer. But she would not give him false hope.

She flashed him a coy smile instead and kissed his thighs 'I've been doing some thinking about our last night on the road,' she said. 'I've concluded that what is good for the goose is good for the gander.' She moved her hand over the fall of his trousers and cupped the tip of him, watching his jaw tighten against the pleasure it brought him. 'You're going to be stubborn...' she wet her lips '... I should have known.' Stubborn, stoic, serious. Those would always be parts of Inigo Vellanoweth, those things that protected the powder-keg kisses and the passions that threatened to rule him if he gave them free rein. Many men did. But Inigo was made of sterner stuff and that would make tonight's victory that much more delightful. Tonight, she would have him once more for all time.

'You are wearing entirely too many clothes. Let me remedy that.' She worked his trousers down past his lean hips, his smallclothes following. 'I'd rather you did without these,' she said, freeing him to her hand at last. 'And they say women wear too many clothes. Hah.' He was warm to her touch and hard... oh, so hard—proof that despite his outward show of stoicism, he was aroused by her and easily. The merest contact of her hand, her mouth, had him hard and wanting. She would remember that: that a good man had desired her.

'Your hand is magic.' His voice was rough with desire.

'Not just my hand.' She gave him a wicked look, watching his own face change as he understood her.

'Aud, you don't need to,' he said. 'It's different for men. We don't expect ladies to reciprocate.'

'Then prepare to be surprised.' She licked her lips. 'Why should you have all the fun? All the pleasure? I want to.' Her own voice was low and hoarse. 'And I wanted you to feel what I felt when your mouth was on me.' She saw his throat clench, the muscles of his neck working hard and then she bent to him, her mouth taking him at his tip, her lips kissing his length before returning to the tender top of him, her ministrations bolder now as she sucked at him, tasting his saltiness. Her hand worked him in tandem, her entire body revelling in his response—the tightness of his muscles, the way his neck arched and his hands gripped the arms of the chair, digging into the fabric until they hit wood, the sounds he made in the back of his throat, guttural and primal as his body slowly ceded to pleasure.

'Aud,' he rasped her name in warning. She could feel the little changes in him as his release approached. She gave a final pull at his tip and sat back on her heels, catching him in her hand as he spilled himself over her fingers. She watched his face, riveted by how he took his pleasure, how it ripped from

him. It might be the most vulnerable, the most exposed she'd ever seen him, his guard entirely down.

She rose and stepped back, pulling her pink gown
over her head, leaving herself naked to his gaze.
'How long do you think it will be before you can
take me to bed?'

'Not too long.' Inigo stood, as if in testimony to
his words, and strode towards her, swinging her up
in his arms and carrying her to the big bed. He followed her down with a growl. 'At this rate, you are
going to be the death of me.'

No, she wouldn't. That was the whole point of
this.

Inigo awoke sated, letting himself enjoy the slow
rise to morning's surface that comes after a night
of lovemaking. He was in no hurry to embrace the
day and the realities that came with it, not while
the memory of Audevere's sweet touch was still im-
printed on his mind and his body. He wanted to drift
in the tide pools of pleasure a while longer.

Inigo flung out an arm, his hand meeting cool
sheets. He was disappointingly but not unexpectedly
alone. Audevere must have gone back to her room in
order to avoid detection from the maids who were up
early to tend the fires. He'd slept deeply, so deeply
he'd not heard her stir, much to his detriment. He
would have liked to have had her once more before
dawn. Or was that he would have liked her to have

had him once more? Audevere was a precocious, inexhaustible lover and in that they were well matched.

They were well matched in other ways, too. Both protectors, both with a deep capacity to love that they often hid behind strong exteriors, unwilling to make themselves appear vulnerable to the outside world. He saw those qualities in her now and it amazed him that he hadn't seen them before, all those years ago.

Inigo threw back the covers and rang for his valet. There was much to settle today, starting with target practice, and all of it moved him one step closer to claiming Audevere. It was motive enough to get out of bed.

Shaved and dressed, Inigo made his way to the breakfast room. He smiled at his family as he assembled his plate from the sideboard. 'Audevere isn't down yet?' he asked, spooning a large serving of eggs on to his plate. Perhaps it was no surprise she'd slept late if she was as sated as he was from lovemaking.

'No.' Mary Rose shook her head, her pink hair ribbon catching Inigo's eye. 'I am hoping she can help me trim my green dress today.'

'Where did you get that ribbon?' He took a seat next to Sarah and noted she wore a similar one.

Sarah touched the bow. 'Audevere gave them to us yesterday. Isn't it the loveliest silk?'

It was also very sentimental. He couldn't imagine why Audevere would have cut up her length of ribbon after what she'd told him in the coach. Unless… Unless she'd finally realised he would take care of her, that she need not want for anything. For a moment something akin to joy buoyed within him, only to be overtaken by a darker feeling. Or unless she'd been saying goodbye. A flash back to the past took him unawares. He remembered that last day with Collin. Collin had wanted to give him something, a polished rock. It wasn't expensive, but they'd found it on the beach when they were children and for a long time they'd believed it was a pirate's gold nugget. It had become a token of their friendship, a physical memory of their childhood. It had meaning only to them.

Inigo rose, fighting back a wave of panic. 'I think I'll just go and check on her to make sure she's well.' Once out of the breakfast room, he took the stairs two at a time, hoping he was wrong. He had to be wrong. She was just sleeping late. But all the signs that pointed to her contentment here also pointed to farewell. He suddenly saw yesterday in a different light. Her reticence to accept his proposal, her determination to spend the afternoon with the girls and Ben, offering them gifts in her own way. Coming to his room last night, not as a sign of committing to him, but as a leave-taking. One last night of passion.

He knocked at her door and then barged in, modesty and propriety be damned. But there was no one inside to offend. Her room was empty. She was gone. He could feel it. The room felt sterile, devoid of her vitality already. He looked for clues anyway, hoping he was wrong. Her borrowed dresses hung in the wardrobe, but her own clothes were nowhere to be found. He felt a presence behind him and turned in the hope that it would be her. It was not.

His father stood in the doorway. 'Is she gone? I'm sorry, Son.'

'Why would she do this? She knew I meant to marry her, to make things right for her and for us,' Inigo said, casting about in his mind for a narrative that explained this divergence. 'I want to talk to the servants. I want to know who saw her last.' His mind began to make plans. 'I'll go after her and bring her back.'

His father put a steadying hand on his arm. 'You will *think* first and act second. Right now, you're acting on impulse.' Damn right he was, every moment that passed put Audevere further from him. There was no time…

'You will go downstairs, you will eat your breakfast and then you will question the servants and your sisters—perhaps she told them something yesterday—and then we'll decide what's to be done, if anything.'

Inigo shot his father an incredulous look. 'If anything?'

'Son, she may not want to be followed. I know it's not the answer you want to hear, but it might be the truth.' But that truth was not acceptable to Inigo.

It made no sense, not after last night, not after the promises their bodies had made one another. Something was wrong.

Chapter Twenty-One

Why wouldn't she want to be followed? Why would she leave in the first place? Inigo chased those two questions around in his head as he forced down his breakfast, listening to his sisters talk through the previous afternoon, his attentions finally finding something to grab on to in Mary Rose's words.

'I was looking for her to help with hair braids,' Mary Rose said. 'I found her in the alcove by Father's office. She looked upset, as though she'd been crying. She was pale, too, as though she'd been scared.'

'What time was that?' Inigo exchanged a look with his father. They'd been closeted away in conversation most of the afternoon discussing Brenley's letter.

'Three o'clock,' Mary Rose offered, furrowing her brow. 'Did you say something to frighten her?' She was quick to jump to her new friend's defence and it warmed Inigo even in the midst of a crisis. Audevere would have a family here who loved her if he could only get her back.

'I might have. *We* might have.' He held his father's gaze, looking for concurrence. 'We were discussing the actions to take regarding her father. We didn't say anything to her, but perhaps she overheard us talking.' Inigo replayed the conversation in his mind, trying to hear it from her point of view. Had she heard them discuss going to the King with direct exposure? Had she heard them discuss the propensity for a duel? If she had, she'd be mortified. She'd try to stop it any way she could. Inigo's hand froze around his coffee cup as he recalled their exchange last night, playful and intimate though it had seemed at the time: 'You'll be the death of me,' he'd said. She'd laughed at him and replied silkily, 'I hope not.' But she'd meant it as more than a flirty rejoinder.

She'd left to protect him. Her father could not force a wedding to a bride who was missing. 'She didn't leave because she doesn't love me, but because she does.' Inigo looked at his father. 'She doesn't want to be followed; you're right about that. But not for the reasons you think. She must have overheard us talking and decided to take matters into her own hands.' Of course she had. Audevere was used to being alone, acting alone. It stung that she didn't quite trust the togetherness of them yet, but he understood it. If given the chance to protect her through his absence, he might have chosen the same.

He rose, already issuing orders for his horse and for a bag to be packed. 'I'm going after her. It's time

Audevere understands she doesn't always get what she wants.'

'Where do you suppose she is? You don't know where to look. It could be a wild goose chase,' his father cautioned. 'I'll come with you. Perhaps two heads are better than one in this case. Or perhaps you should wait for Eaton?'

Inigo declined the offer with a shake of his head. 'No, I need you here to send the letter to the King. It must go at once and send word to Eaton, although it will all be over before Eaton can be of any help. If she overheard us talking, she'll head to Truro. Her father's there.' Inigo wished she'd chosen to head back to Exeter, though. It would be safer for her, but only if she meant to disappear. She could vanish from the big city without much notice, but simply disappearing was no longer what she was after. She wanted to stop the duel and, to do that, she had to go to her father. Heaven only knew what might happen if her father got his hands on her, or what sort of deal Audevere might be compelled to make to save Inigo's life. But Audevere was never one to choose the easy path and now she'd chosen to walk into the lion's den. He had no choice but to follow her. That was how it worked when a man was in love. He was going to bring her back and he was going to end the feud with Brenley once and for all.

She was going to end this once and for all. Audevere rapped on the town-house door with a determination summoned by the remainder of her courage. She'd already spent a great part of it in leaving Inigo, in catching the mail coach and making the journey to Truro, which had taken the better part of the morning and early afternoon, sitting squeezed beside a parson and his wife. She'd had a lot of time for thoughts and second thoughts.

'Yes, ma'am?' the butler asked by rote, before recognition sank in. 'Miss Brenley, please come in.' The butler did his duty, but eyed her speculatively. 'I didn't know we were expecting you.' He led her to the drawing room.

'Please tell my father I am here and have some tea sent.' Whatever happened, it was not going to happen on an empty stomach. She'd not eaten since dinner last night and she was beginning to feel the effects. Her father was making her wait, no doubt punishing her for her truancy. She rehearsed her lines, not sure of the reception she'd receive. Her gaze drifted around the room and into the hallway past the open doors. She sensed a difference in the town house. There was a quiet bustle to it, something furtive. The drawing room itself seemed emptier. Did she imagine it, or were the table tops devoid of their expensive clutter?

She strolled to the window and looked down into the street, searching faces. But for what? Who did she expect to see? Inigo? Would he come after her? She hoped not. It would defeat the purpose of having left him. She wanted him nowhere near her father.

But the beat of her heart felt differently. She had not wanted to leave him, but it was simply the only way. They could not be together and live without fear of her father. He would always be a threat to Inigo and a threat to their happiness. It had broken her heart to leave him, but she loved him too much to ruin him.

She wondered what he'd thought this morning? Was he railing against her even now, full of anger and rage? Or had he accepted that despite what they wanted, it was impossible to be together? Rival families didn't marry into one another. It hadn't worked for Romeo and Juliet and it wouldn't work for her, especially since the Brenleys weren't grand enough to be true rivals of the Vellanoweths, merely enemies.

'What an unexpected surprise this is,' her father drawled from the doorway. He fussed with his cuffs, making sure just the right length of white shirt peeped out from beneath his jacket sleeve. He looked urbane and confident, entirely in control. 'May I surmise you are here because the young Earl is done with you? Or are you his messenger? Has he sent you to tell me that his letter had gone forward to the King and soon I will be stripped of my title?' he sneered, his tone bitter. 'He will die for his honour and for besmirching mine.'

'I came to offer you a way out. Leave here and never look back. Your assets are portable. You can leave with your wealth intact and I will go with you, just leave Inigo and the Dukes alone. You can't think to escape detection if that letter comes out and suddenly Inigo Vellanoweth is shot fatally.' She hoped her argument was cogent. She felt rumpled and exhausted.

Her father laughed. 'Do you think I've not already thought of that? How nice of you to offer yourself in exchange for my leaving. But I've already decided leaving is in my best interest. No deal, though. I absolutely do not promise to leave the young Earl alone.'

He leaned against the door jamb as if this were a pleasant conversation. 'I have to say, I'm a little disappointed he didn't come himself and give me the pleasure of shooting him for all the trouble he's caused me. But...' he brightened '...perhaps not all is lost. I would have hated to leave you behind, my dear.' His eyes looked her up and down, appraising. 'Even if your value to me is somewhat diminished. But no one in Russia needs to know that.'

'Russia?' Audevere glanced furtively towards the doorway.

'We're going east, to Russia. I have extensive interests there and I think the Baltic may be the next big thing, if southern Europe persists in its warlike tendencies.' He crossed one leg over the other. 'Do you fancy yourself a prince for a husband? I am sure we can find one willing to wed you and I can advance my position at the St Petersburg court.' That explained the empty table tops. Servants were indeed packing. Her instincts had not been wrong. 'Don't worry, my dear, much of this will follow us once we're settled.' He was indeed leaving in a very permanent way. He levelled his gaze in her direction. 'Inigo Vellanoweth has ruined England for me for a while. It seems you didn't have him quite as much under your control as we thought.' He lifted a brow in scolding inquiry. 'Care to tell me what happened there? No, don't. I can already guess. You fell for him, all that dark, persuasive charm. You thought you could escape me, perhaps even abet him in my complete ruin.'

Her father strode to the remaining decanter and poured a drink. But she was not fooled by his sang-froid. She was distressed by it. He was never more dangerous than when he was charming someone or acting as if he admired their cunning. 'Don't worry, my dear, we will find some way for you to make it up to me.'

Briefly, she wondered what her chances were of making it to the front door. Her father gave her a cool smile. 'You won't make the door. I have men already posted. You are not leaving here, except with me, tonight. Or...' he sighed, affecting boredom '... I suppose, if Vellanoweth wants you, he can try to claim you.' Her father mused cruelly, 'Did he promise you marriage? Did you think he meant it or was he just playing with you? Perhaps some payback for his dead friend? Surely you weren't stupid enough to fall for that? In the end he had to tattle to the King like a pathetic schoolboy.'

He tossed back the rest of the drink and poured

another, emptying the decanter. 'You can pack this now,' he called to the butler.

'So, Daughter,' he said with feigned affability, 'do you think he'll come for you? I do. I am counting on it, in fact. The only question is how easy did you make it for him to find you? I hope easy enough before the boat sails tonight. I'd like a shot at him.'

Audevere stiffened. 'It's a long way from Boscastle to Truro.' Perhaps that distance would protect him. Surely her father didn't mean to kill him?

'Then let's hope he got an early start and let's hope he's smart enough not to go to Exeter or he'll miss you entirely, early start or not.'

'Why would he go to Exeter?' The words left her slowly, a cold chill tightening her stomach.

Her father faced her. 'Haven't you figured it out yet? After all these years? That despite your disobedience, you've played into my hand spectacularly. Once Vellanoweth put his gambit in motion to stop me I knew it was only matter of time until you came.' Her father wandered to the chessboard set laid out on a table against the wall and pushed a pawn forward. 'He exposes me to the King, I am forced to defend my honour or admit to extraordinary guilt that will result in losing my title.'

He moved a bishop into play. 'In a duel, Vellanoweth has the advantage with rapiers or with pistols. He's one of the best swordsmen in the city and rumour has it he's been shooting out centres of wafers ad nauseum at Manton's.' He moved a rook, creeping up behind the bishop. 'But you know this. Perhaps you fear for your lover regardless of his expertise, or perhaps you don't want to start the promise of married life under a cloud of murder.' He shrugged. 'So, once it became apparent that duelling was my only recourse, the trap for you was sprung. You come running to me, begging me to reconsider. Am I right?'

She hated that for all her efforts to be free, she was more enslaved than she'd ever been. His next words froze her. 'I don't mind the shooting,' he said casually. 'I only mind when someone can shoot back. I hope he comes for you. I hope you're right and that he does love you. Nothing will keep him from you then; he's the sort of man who is willing to die for a woman he loves and that will be his undoing. We'll be waiting for him and we'll be ready. By the end of today, Inigo Vellanoweth will be dead and his last thought will be that he'll wish he had never crossed Sir Gismond Brenley. He might succeed in taking my title, but I will succeed in taking his life. I wonder if he will consider that a fair trade?' He nodded towards a footman. 'Help Miss Brenley to her room and make sure she stays there. She might enjoy the company of a maid while she waits.'

Chapter Twenty-Two

Would she never learn? Audevere stared at the street from her bedroom window with morbid fascination, wanting to see Inigo the moment he arrived, yet hoping for his own sake he didn't arrive. This was Collin all over again. She had tried to save him by breaking with him. She'd tried to save Inigo, too, by running from him, but it had only served to create a trap for him. If he knocked on the town-house door now, he would be shot the moment the door opened. Would he be so bold as to simply stroll up to the door? Or would he effect reconnaissance? Would he suspect anything? How could he suspect anything?

She had tried to help, tried to protect him, and she'd only made it worse. The one consolation was that the hours ticked by and there was no sign of Inigo. He wasn't coming. Either because he'd guessed her destination incorrectly or because he'd decided it was over, that she was too much trouble, or that she didn't want him after all.

The downstairs clock, which wasn't going to travel with them, it seemed, struck four and her door opened. It was time to go. The ship was waiting. Inigo was nearly safe. Once the ship was out of the quay, he would be. Going peaceably with her father bought Inigo's safety. The faster they embarked, the better in that regard. But her heart was breaking all the same and she knew her father had devised this dilemma on purpose to teach her a lesson. Only once the boat was out of the harbour would she have to address the question of why Inigo hadn't come.

There was a cloak waiting for her and she threw it on against the late afternoon chill. She went to put the hood up, only to be stalled. 'No hood, let him have every chance to see you.' Her father smiled coldly. 'Although I must say I'm disappointed. This leave-taking is far less dramatic than it might have been. I feel robbed of my due, don't you, my dear?'

More than that. She felt robbed of what might have been. She'd had a real chance to trust, to love, to have a family, and she'd lost it, all to her own machinations. She had done this to herself. She'd got exactly what she'd deserved.

Inigo banged on the town-house door. He'd ridden hard through mud, stopping in Bodmin to change horses, knowing time was against him. Boscastle was not an easy ride to Truro and now at the end of the journey there was no one to greet him. The town house, in fact, looked deserted. It had a closed-up feel to it, which made no sense since it had been clear from his letter that Brenley was in residence. Finally, he stood in the street and called up, 'Audevere!' But there was no answer to that either.

'Sir, there's no one home. They've gone, an hour or more ago.' An apple vendor took pity on him. Inigo stared. The boy must think him a lunatic.

'What do you mean gone?' There were all types of gone. There was paying calls, there was going shopping, and then there was gone as in fled, gone beyond reach.

'Trunks have been leaving the house all morning and then a girl showed up and more trunks left, and then at four, they left,' the vendor recited, holding out his palm.

Inigo pressed a coin into it and then added another. 'Any idea where they went?' There were only two ways out of Truro, the road or by sea.

'I'm guessing they went to the quay. There's a ship that's been loading all day and is set to sail on the tide. There were too many trunks for a carriage.'

Inigo nodded his thanks, already leaping back into the saddle of a tired horse and putting his heels to its sides. Another twenty minutes and the tide would be in, boats would sail and he'd be too late despite his best efforts. He'd cursed himself the whole way. Why hadn't he woken up sooner? Why hadn't he set out sooner? Why hadn't he seen this coming and stopped it? Why hadn't he ridden faster? A few minutes might make all the difference.

* * *

The quay was bustling with activity, the crowd working against him. There was more than one ship and no way of knowing which one they would be on. How would he find her in this crush? How did he free her from Brenley? Inigo grabbed a carter by the coat sleeve. 'That boat there, where is it going?' He pointed to the largest ship in the harbour.

'It's going through the Channel up to Denmark and then through the Baltic. It won't be back for a year.' That was the ship. Inigo knew it in his gut. Brenley's holdings, Brenley's dealings with the Russian court. He would take refuge far from England until the scandal blew itself out. At the ship, a sailor was untying mooring lines.

Inigo raced towards it, looking for signs of Audevere, trying not to trip over coils of rope, trying to dodge the crowd. He caught a glimpse of golden hair at the railing. There she was! 'Audevere!' he called her name, waving frantically. It only mattered that he got her attention, that he could get her off the ship. He reached the gangplank, yelling for the men to hold it. He bounded up the ramp, his pistol drawn, only to have his way barred by Gismond Brenley and a loaded gun. They levelled their pistols at one another, locked in a deadly stalemate. To shoot at this range would be certain death for either of them.

'I've informed the captain you are not to board this boat. I will shoot you if I have to.' Brenley's eyes locked with his. 'Do I make myself clear? Try to board this ship, try to take Audevere from it, and I will shoot you dead where you stand.' Inigo knew when to take a threat seriously. Brenley *wanted* an excuse to shoot him. It would be an expedient remedy to the situation.

'No!' There was a cry behind Brenley as Audevere flew towards them, her face pale with panic and fear—fear for him as she put herself between him and her father. Inigo's heart was in his throat at all she'd risked for him, to save him, misguided though it was. What was she thinking, to put herself between hot tempers and primed pistols? But he knew what she was thinking and he knew, too, that he'd been right to come, right to believe she'd thought to protect him with her flight. Had anyone ever risked so much for him? That it should be the woman he loved touched him more than he could find words to express. But today was his day to save her. If only he could get her to stand aside.

'Aud, get out of the way,' Inigo warned.

'No, I will not step aside and let him kill you.' She did not turn to look at him, but spoke directly to her father. 'I offer you my deal once more. I will go with you, do what you want, if you let him live. Let him go.'

'No, Aud!' Inigo growled.

Brenley's lip curled. 'But will he go?' he mused out loud. 'I wonder, Audevere, if *he* will take that deal? Will you, Tintagel? Will you walk away and leave her? Tsk, tsk, I see you're already looking for ways to circumvent the terms. Well, I'll tell you what. I've always been interested in the things we do for love. So, I'll take that offer. I'll let you live, Tintagel. Now, walk away.'

'I will not leave her. You don't deserve her.' Inigo was already wondering if he could make the shot over her shoulder, just enough to incapacitate Brenley, enough to get her away.

She turned and walked a little way towards him. *Inigo, go*, she pleaded with her eyes.

'I'll make it easy on you, Tintagel,' Brenley called, lifting his pistol once more. 'I only promised not to shoot you. I said nothing about her.'

'Aud!' Inigo yelled the warning, his body gathering into motion, but he was too late to stop the shot. Brenley's pistol fired, catching Audevere in the shoulder, the force of it knocking her off balance, sending her into the depths of the cold waters of the harbour.

From a crouch, he raised his own pistol, his mind a riot of thoughts: disarm Brenley, prevent him from shooting again, dive in after Audevere, bring her to the surface… But the ship's captain was already ahead of him, moving to detain Brenley. 'Go, get the girl!' the captain yelled. Inigo didn't wait to pull off his boots, he dived into the water after her, but she'd disappeared from sight.

The harbour water was dark and cold as it closed over his head. Inigo forced his eyes open. There! He caught a glimpse of floating fabric, dark and colourless as the water, but the golden hair was a beacon. He swam towards it, the form limp, as the water pinkened about her. She was bleeding and unconscious. Fear gave him strength. He could not be too late! An edge of her heavy cloak was trapped in some rocks. He tore the cloak from Audevere's still form and hooked an arm about her waist before beginning the long rise to the surface. Men were waiting, drawn to the commotion. Hands reached over the dock to pull them out of the water, Audevere first, still lifeless, still bleeding.

Inigo scrambled to her side; she was so pale, so cold. He lifted her in his arms, calling orders as he went. 'Get a blanket, get a doctor! She's been shot, for heaven's sake!' Her bastard father had shot her to prove a point, to win a game. This could not be how it ended. It couldn't be. He loved her. He tore at his sodden cravat and pressed it against her wound. He had to stop the bleeding, had to make her breath. So much to do, so little time! How long could a person live without air? How much blood could a person lose? How long would it take for a doctor to arrive? In his despair, he rocked her against him, holding her upright. Suddenly she coughed, harbour water gushing from her lungs as she fought for air in panicked gasps. 'It's all right, it's all right,' Inigo repeated the inane words and held her tight until the spasms subsided.

Someone brought a blanket and he drew it around her. 'Aud—oh, my sweet Aud. I thought I'd lost you.

What a foolish thing to do, my love. A doctor is coming, you will be fine.'

Inigo looked up to see Brenley being shackled and led away.

The doctor arrived at last and did a cursory examination of the wound. 'The bullet has passed through, we just need to stitch her up and keep the wound clean. Can you get her to the inn? They'll have a room ready.'

She was shaking from cold, from shock, from the wound, as he scooped her up in his arms, his own strength running on reserves because she required it of him. At the inn, someone pressed a hot drink into his hand and offered him dry clothes, but he would not leave Audevere, never mind that she drifted in and out of consciousness as the doctor stitched her shoulder. She needed him to hold her hand, to murmur comfort, to see her into dry clothes and a warm bed. Then, and only then, did Inigo see to himself.

Only after that, when he was able to lie next to her in the bed, did he let the horror of the day have its way with him. Now that she was safe, it was his turn to shake with the horror of the last few hours. He held her a long while as she slept. It was what he wanted to do, to assure himself that she was alive, that they were both alive, his mind fixated on one awful refrain: the woman he loved had stood between him and a bullet today. And they still weren't out of the woods yet.

The fever started at midnight. The doctor had alerted him to the possibility and Inigo strove to control it with wet rags and by throwing off the covers. This was a likely and natural course of events, he told himself as he laid another cool cloth over Audevere's forehead. He would bring the fever down and it would be gone by morning.

But the fever continued to rise, battling back against his efforts with cold cloths.

By dawn, Audevere was burning and restless and Inigo worried for her shoulder. When the sun came up, he sent for the doctor, wanting answers and fixes and getting neither while Audevere burned.

'Fever means inflammation,' the doctor told him as he checked and redressed Audevere's shoulder, 'although I don't see any sign of it. The wound looks clean and the bullet went through. The other possibility is a fever from her fall into the water. She was under long enough, the water cold enough, to give her quite a chill.' The doctor put his instruments away and snapped his bag shut. 'There's nothing to do now but wait for the fever to break.' He put a bracing hand on Inigo's sleeve. 'She's already delirious. If it continues to rise, it will burn her alive.'

Inigo nodded. He didn't need to be told how dangerous a high fever was, how it could damage the brain, the heart. Even if one woke up, one could be severely impaired for life. He'd seen two infant siblings slip into fever's grasp. But Audevere wasn't an infant and she was young and strong. Surely a fever could not take her, not after all she'd endured? He thanked the doctor and sent down to the taproom for more cold compresses before he shut the door behind him. He faced the bed, hands on hips, his sleeves already rolled up, prepared to do battle.

He laboured through the morning with cold baths administered with chilled rags, sips of water and with his words. He talked non-stop. He remembered his mother doing that when the babies had taken ill. She'd rocked them and talked to them endlessly, hoping the sound of her voice would keep them anchored to this world. He hoped for that now with Audevere, that the sound of his voice would reach her, would draw her back. He told her everything he could think of: how her father was even now chained up in jail and would be put on trial for his crimes, how he'd felt when he'd discovered she'd fled, how much the girls had exclaimed over her pink ribbon.

He talked until he was hoarse and aware of his own strength faltering. He'd not slept last night and he'd barely taken time to eat. He was going to need reinforcements. He sent a hasty note by courier to Merry Weather, three hours away. This battle would not be over in a morning, or even in a day as he'd thought twelve hours ago. On the bed, Audevere lay pale and sweating, babbling nonsense in the grip of the fever. He applied more cold compresses, but felt more impotent each time. The fever seemed to burn right through them, turning the rags warm as soon as they touched her skin.

By late afternoon, impotence had turned to guilt. This was his fault. She'd wanted to simply disappear and he hadn't let her. He had insisted they could do more, have more, that they could challenge Brenley and it had led to this. She was beyond him once more.

Chapter Twenty-Three

Tここ was a knock at the door shortly after supper time and, for a brief moment, Inigo's hope surged. He answered the door and found Eaton standing there, tall, imposing, surely a bulwark against all evil, supplies from home slung over his back. 'Eaton, she's burning up.' His own voice was a rasp.

Eaton set the pack down on the table. 'Your mother sent willow bark tea to bring down the fever if you can get her to drink it. Your mother said to rub her feet to draw the fever down and then try wet stockings.' He put a hand on Inigo's shoulder. 'Everyone sends their love. I'm glad I arrived in time to be of help. I must have arrived at Merry Weather but an hour before your note came.' He'd come because a council of the Cornish Dukes had been called, but now such a summons seemed pointless.

'She's not doing well,' Inigo confessed, pushing a hand through his hair in frustration.

'Perhaps the tea and the wet stockings will help.

Don't give up. Meanwhile, you look like hell. I have strict instructions from your mother to take care of you as well. Dinner is on its way up, along with a cot. You will eat and you will sleep. I will watch Aude-vere and wake you if anything changes.'

Inigo smiled for the first time in days. 'You always were the one to take care of all of us.'

'Looks like nothing has changed.' Eaton grinned. 'Now, I'll lay out dinner while you brew the tea.'

It took both of them to get any tea into her; one to hold her upright and another to carefully manoeuvre the cup into position to reduce dribbling, but even after fifteen minutes of careful effort, she'd only managed to swallow half a cup. 'We'll try again after supper.' Inigo set aside the cup and went to the table. Eaton had ordered a hearty soup and fresh bread, but Inigo had to force the food down.

'You have to try, too,' Eaton insisted when Inigo ate only half a bowl. 'You cannot help her if you take ill as well.'

Inigo speared him with a hard look. 'Platitudes, Eaton? Is that the best you've got? How can I eat when I look at her? Every hour she slips further away and it's my fault. I pushed her to this. I pushed her to believe we could fight Brenley, that I could keep her safe. All she wanted was to disappear and start over, but I had to go and try to change her mind. I might as well have pulled the trigger myself.' Inigo pushed back from the table with a force that sent the chair slamming against the wall, his anger breaking free. 'Dammit all! Audevere was never meant for me. I wasn't supposed to have her.' Agony ripped through him at the admission. This was at the core of what haunted him. They were not meant to be and now she would die because he'd tempted fate.

He leaned his head against the wall and let the pain of his guilt take him. Why hadn't he ridden faster? Why hadn't he woken up sooner, why hadn't he realised she was going to leave? Why hadn't he just shot Brenley at the docks? What was his life worth if Audevere died?

Eaton was beside him, his voice quiet. 'Oh, Inigo, you do have a heart after all, don't you? The quiet ones are always the ones who feel the most, isn't that what the old wives say?'

'I love her. I would do anything for her, even give her up.' Inigo raised his gaze to meet Eaton's steady eyes. 'I've already given her up once, you know. I suppose I can do it again. I let Collin have her because he saw her first. I never told anyone. I loved her from the first moment I saw her, but she wasn't mine to love so I hid it, from all of you, perhaps even from myself.' Tears made slow streaks down his face, his breath came in barely controlled gasps. He had only a little control left; his body wanted to rage, wanted to howl. 'It shamed me for years that I wanted her. If she would only live, I would give her up, I'd let her go away as she wanted.' He'd let her do anything, go anywhere. It would be enough to know that she was in the world, some place.

Eaton had a brandy in his hand, a gesture reminiscent of Richard Penlerick's funeral. Inigo remembered how Eaton had pressed a sustaining glass into Vennor's hand. 'Drink, and then sleep. Just an hour or two. You're worn out—that's why you're talking like this. You have to stay strong for her. She needs you,' Eaton insisted.

They sat on the cot together, brandies in hand. 'You know, I had a fever when I came out of the mine with Eliza in my arms, my shoulder shot to bits,' Eaton said. 'My situation was not unlike Audevere's.' Inigo remembered. Until now, he'd never been more frightened in his life than the night someone had left Eliza Blaxland in her own mine to die. Eaton had gone in after her and been shot for his efforts. He'd lingered with a fever for days until everyone had begun to fear the worst.

'Peace is what is tempting her now.' Eaton met his gaze with a sideways glance. 'There are no worries on the other side. There is light and there is peace and there is no pain. I could never have children of my own, I could never give Eliza the big family she dreamed of. How could I condemn her to life with a sterile man? But without Eliza, what did I have to live for? No family of my own. No one needed me. Not even the succession needed me. I had my younger brother to carry that on. Why not slip away? I thought. Why not let go and set Eliza free once she was safe? Once I knew you and Cassian and Vennor would take care of her, keep her safe from Brenley, what did I have to live for? I'd nearly convinced myself slipping away was best.'

'But you didn't,' Inigo interrupted. Eaton had never talked of that time, had never talked of his impairment, his sterility from a measles epidemic in his adolescence. Inigo never would have guessed how close they'd all come to losing Eaton or why. 'I'm glad. We could never have done without you, Eaton. You're our leader, our caretaker.'

'No, I didn't, because Eliza came to me and poured out her heart. I could hear her and she called me back. I know it sounds like magic, like fairy tales. I'm a scientist, I believe in medicines, yet that's what saved me when medicines failed.'

'I've talked to her,' Inigo protested.

'Try again, after you've slept,' Eaton encouraged.

Inigo had not meant to sleep and certainly not for as long as he did. Except for the fire, the room was dark when Eaton shook him awake with urgency. 'She needs you, Inigo. I think it's now or never.'

Inigo raced to her side, her hand searing him with its heat, panic flooding him.

'God, Aud, you have to wake up, you have to break this fever.'

He rubbed her hand. Did she truly think there was no reason to wake up? That there was no future for them?

'Aud, we have a wedding to plan, a life to build,'

Inigo said, words giving shape to his dreams as he gave her his heart, his soul. 'Aud, come back to me, I love you.'

'Aud, come back to me, I love you.'
The words halted her in her tracks. The light at the end of the path seemed to shrink. She turned, squinting her eyes back along the grey road. What was back there? Who was calling to her? Who loved her? Not her father. She'd heard his voice often enough on this grey journey.

'Bastard. No one will want you if they know what you really are, the natural-born daughter of a French actress. You are nothing but what I allow you to be. How dare you defy me? You are nothing but a pawn, my chess piece to move about the board as I choose.'

Somewhere deep inside her, she'd always known that to be the truth. No matter how much she laughed and flirted and danced with gentlemen and wore fine dresses, she was always nothing, just a captain's daughter from Truro, and in truth she was not even really that. She was a captain's bastard. Not even her mother was her own. She was nothing, she had nothing. Until she'd met Inigo…

'Aud, I love you.'
She'd not imagined it. She turned back into the grey tentatively, intrigued. The words were an echo now, repeating and repeating.

'Aud, I love you…your beautiful body…your beau-

*tiful soul that cares enough about justice to leave
everything behind to save others...to stand between
me and a bullet. Come back to me...marry me...be
my wife...raise our children with me...help the people of Cornwall rise against corruption…help me
rise. I will be nothing without you. Please, Audevere, help me rise…'*

She was running now through grey mist, hurrying
towards the voice. Where was Inigo? He was in pain,
she heard it in his voice, this man who commanded
the world effortlessly, who bowed to no one. But he
was bowing to her, breaking because of her. 'Inigo!'
she called to him, but her voice had disappeared.
How would he hear her? She wanted to look at him,
to see his face with its pale-blue eyes, but her own
eyes seemed to be glued shut, too heavy to lift. Even
running was an effort, her legs leaden on the path
she'd flown down. She summoned her voice again.
'Inigo, I am here.' It was a cracked whisper, nothing
more. She forced herself to move, each step an effort. 'Inigo, I am coming. Don't break. I am coming.'

One more step and then another. Her eyes began
to lift and she was there, looking up into the pale-
blue eyes of the man she loved, the man who loved
her, and he was weeping. The strongest man she'd
ever known was weeping for her. 'Inigo, I'm back,'
she whispered with the last of her voice. She didn't
need it any more, not now at any rate. She was in
his arms, bodily lifted from the bed and into his lap
as he rocked her, calling for water, calling for broth,

calling for a doctor. Silly man, didn't he know she didn't need any of those things? She just needed him.

'Aud, you scared the life out of me.' Inigo held her close and she was in no hurry for him to let go. This was what she'd come back for. 'When you fell, you disappeared into the water and I couldn't see you. All I could think about was getting to you and not even that was enough. You seemed determined to leave me.'

He'd been truly frightened, but even in his fright he'd been the bravest, strongest man she'd ever known. He'd fought for her, for them, every step of the way, even when she'd been determined to give up. She lifted a hand to his cheek. 'Thank you for never giving up. I love you, Inigo.' It was the first time she'd ever said the words to anyone, the first time she'd ever said them to him and she wished she hadn't waited so long. She'd nearly lost the chance to say them at all.

Inigo was careful with her in the days that followed, encouraging her to rest, making sure she didn't overtax herself. He read to her and stayed at her bedside. There were plenty of *I love you*s, plenty of kisses exchanged between them, but she knew those words weren't enough to resolve what still lay between them. 'What happened to my father?' she asked on the third day when it was apparent that Inigo wasn't going to bring it up for fear of worrying her. Had Inigo been forced to shoot him? Had he sailed off, once more unaccountable for his crimes?

'He's being held,' Inigo offered slowly. 'Waiting on the King's pleasure to decide his fate.'

'You sent the letter, then?' Audevere shifted on her pillows, trying to get comfortable. Her energy was returning and she was less than an ideal patient now. She was eager to be out and about, but where? Would they go back to Merry Weather? Could they pick up the pieces of what they might have had? Or did she need to carry on with her plan and disappear?

'Yes. We should hear shortly what his fate will be.' Inigo reached for her hand. 'But I am more interested in deciding our fate. I almost lost you. I don't want to wait any longer, for other things to be decided. My happiness, and yours, doesn't deserve to be contingent on anything else but us. I want to marry you before autumn is out, so that I can celebrate the holidays at Merry Weather with my wife.'

'You are sure? You want to marry the natural-born daughter of a man who will lose his title and possibly be hanged for attempted murder?'

'No.' Inigo pressed a kiss to her knuckles. 'I want to marry you, Audevere, just you. Not your past. Not your father's crimes. It's time to let the past stop defining us both.' He leaned in and kissed her on the mouth. 'It's time for us to burn the ships, Aud, the whole damn fleet.'

She couldn't agree more.

* * *

It would be a small ceremony at Merry Weather, with only the Dukes, their families and closest friends in attendance. Even so, the family chapel was still rather full on the Wednesday that Aude-vere wed Inigo Vellanoweth, Earl of Tintagel, future Duke of Boscastle. Not that she was in any hurry to become the Duchess. She rather liked her in-laws and they rather liked her, much to her pleasure. The grey skies that had begun that morning had scudded away and a crisp November sky was blue overhead as Audevere stood outside the chapel with her two attendants, Mary Rose and Sarah, both thrilled to be wearing new dresses in the shades of pale-winter rose, lengths of Audevere's pink ribbon threaded through their hair.

She let the girls fuss with her skirts on the stone steps of the chapel while she steadied her nerves. Today, she wore something borrowed and old, Ini-go's mother's own wedding dress, altered to fit in the short weeks of her convalescence. The Duchess, too, it turned out, had been a late autumn bride and the long sleeves and fuller skirts were ideal for the sharp Cornish weather. The gown itself was beau-tiful, trimmed in seed pearls and lace, the fabric a rich, heavy ivory satin. A matching cloak in winter-white wool, trimmed in ermine, lay on the seat for the journey to the wedding breakfast. Something blue was the Boscastle diamond engagement ring Inigo had given her the first night they'd returned to

Merry Weather. There'd been a celebration to rival the name, complete with champagne. As for something new, she carried a bouquet of Eaton's prized orchids straight from the Falmage Hill conservatory. She'd selected each colour carefully for what they symbolised: white for elegance, pink for joy and yellow for new beginnings.

'And a sixpence for your shoe!' Mary Rose cried suddenly. 'Do you have one? Here, take mine,' she insisted just as the doors opened.

'Are you ready?'

Audevere looked up from her shoe to see the Duke of Hayle standing before them. 'Yes.' He still intimidated her. He was Collin's father and she'd not spoken to him alone since the ill-fated engagement years ago.

'You girls go on in, the music has started.' Hayle nodded to Inigo's sisters. 'Remember to walk slowly. It's not a race.' Audevere could hear the strains of the cello-and-violin quartet Inigo had arranged, a lovely Pachelbel's Canon filling the near-winter air. Hayle was looking at her with a smile. 'Would you allow me to give you away?' There was so much unsaid in the kind offer and to have it made by this man who'd lost his son, who might have been her father-in-law had things gone differently, touched her to the core.

'I would be honoured.' She placed her hand on his arm and stepped inside.

Even a small wedding for a duke's heir could fill a chapel, she mused, making her way down the aisle.

The Truscotts were present, the Duchess and Collin's sisters; the Duke of Bude and his wife, along with his younger son; Eaton's wife Eliza and her young daughter, Sophie, and, of course, Inigo's family. At the front of the chapel, Inigo's sisters stood to one side and Eaton stood with Inigo. The altar was simply done in a white cloth, another vase of flowers on it, flanked by two standing candelabra. It was all perfect. But most perfect of all was the man who waited for her.

Inigo stood straight-backed, dressed in a dark-blue morning coat that made his eyes stand out even more intensely, his walnut-dark hair brushed and styled immaculately, his strong jaw fresh shaven. And he was smiling. At her. Only her. Nothing else mattered. Not her birth, not whatever scandal might attach to their marriage—and there would undoubtedly be some. It only mattered that he loved her.

The Duke of Hayle placed her hand in Inigo's and the warm curl of his fingers gripped her hand as he brought it to his lips. 'You are stunning, Aud,' he whispered as the service began, as the rest of her life began. The past was finished and gone. Brenley could do nothing to hurt them now, but in truth, she'd been free the moment Inigo had come for her. His love had freed her in ways that a piece of paper never could. His love had shown her she needn't fear herself. That she was good and kind, and nothing like her father.

'You may kiss the bride,' the vicar intoned. The

service had sped by and now she was moments away from her new life with the most extraordinary of men. Inigo's mouth bent to hers and claimed her with the first kiss of their life together, and she happily gave herself over to it.

Outside, villagers waited to wish them well as they made the short journey from the chapel to the estate and the church bells rang out the news. The Boscastle heir had married, the future looked bright indeed for them all. Inigo threw pennies to the children as they walked the path leading to the wedding breakfast at Merry Weather. At the doorway to the estate, he stole a kiss from her, much to the villagers' delight, and for a few minutes, in the hall, they were alone for the first time as man and wife.

'You make a beautiful bride, Lady Tintagel,' Inigo whispered against her ear. 'When I saw you walk down the aisle, my heart nearly burst to think this woman was mine.'

'I hope you always think that.' She smiled, her own heart too full for words.

'I will. Always. I promise.' He took her hand. 'Are you ready?'

'For what?' Audevere queried.

Inigo grinned. Smiling was coming more easily to him these days. 'To start our happy-ever-after.'

Epilogue

Inigo stood straight-backed on Truro Quay, watching the ship dock, Audevere veiled beside him. He'd waited for this ship to come in for quite some time. Cassian and Pen were coming home today after nearly a year-long honeymoon spent travelling Europe. He'd written ahead to tell Cassian only that he'd married, but he'd not said whom and he'd bade Hayle to say nothing either. He felt this news was best delivered in person. Beside him, he could feel Audevere's nerves as she fidgeted with her veil. This was one last hurdle for them both, to tell Cassian that he'd married his dead brother's fiancée.

It was difficult to think of Audevere as Collin's fiancée, these days. That was part of a past that no longer carried with it guilt and shame. Audevere was his now, as he was hers. He hoped Cassian would see it that way as well. He squeezed Audevere's gloved hand as the gangplank was set. 'They will love you. I haven't been wrong yet.'

He'd not been wrong; his family did love her. And it had immensely helped to grease the wheels of London society, but the Season had been difficult. There were those who'd been more than happy to gossip about her father behind her back. He'd seen to them, of course. Next Season would be better and, in time, everyone would forget about her father. Meanwhile, they were happy together, devoting their days to assisting the poor, to lifting children out of poverty with education. It was a delight to see Audevere working side by side with Eliza to promote not only mining schools, but grammar schools for all children. The last months had been good. Beyond good.

Cassian and Pen stepped on to the quay and Inigo strode forward. 'It's good to see you, old friend.'

'Inigo!' Cassian swept him into a bear hug of an embrace. 'I leave for a few months and you get married.' His voice was as big as his embrace, as big as him in fact. 'I had it on good authority you were not in the market for marriage when I left,' he scolded good-naturedly.

'Hello, Pen, how are you?' Inigo exchanged a much gentler embrace with Cassian's wife.

'Wonderful.' She beamed, exchanging a knowing look with her husband. It was clear the honeymoon magic hadn't worn off yet after nearly a year of marriage. 'We have news, but your news first. Introduce us to your new bride, Inigo.'

'Cassian, Pen, allow me to present Lady Tintagel, Audevere Vellanoweth.'

Audevere drew back her veil and made a curtsy. The shock of recognition was evident in Cassian's eyes. 'You've married Audevere—?'

Inigo cut him off with a sharp look before he could say 'Brenley'. 'Yes, I've married Audevere.'

'I see we all have stories to tell.' Cassian gestured towards a nearby inn. 'I'm starving. Shall we get lunch and swap tales?' It was a good beginning, Inigo thought as they strolled to the inn.

'Before we get into tales,' Cassian said as they took their seats in the private parlour, 'how's Vennor?'

'I think he's in trouble, Cass. But that's a story for another time.' Inigo held out a chair for Audevere. 'Today is for love stories only. You can start with yours and I'll finish with mine.' He took his seat and lifted his mug, his eyes on Audevere. 'A toast to love, the greatest journey of our lifetimes.'

* * * * *